THE THEATRE ON THE PIER

Escaping a disastrous relationship, Llinos Elliot moves to North Wales. There she gets a job as administrator with a children's community theatre, 'The Theatre on the Pier'. Llinos loves her job, and is drawn to Adam Griffiths, the artistic director. But she soon finds her past catching up with her, putting not only her and Adam, but the very existence of the theatre, in danger. Can Llinos overcome her past to find true happiness?

Books by Heather Pardoe
in the Linford Romance Library:

HER SECRET GARDEN
THE IVORY PRINCESS
THE SOARING HEART
THE EAGLE STONE

HEATHER PARDOE

THE THEATRE ON THE PIER

Complete and Unabridged

LINFORD
Leicester

First published in Great Britain in 2006

First Linford Edition
published 2007

British Library CIP Data

Pardoe, Heather
    The theatre on the pier.—Large print ed.—
Linford romance library
    1. Children's theater—Wales, North—Fiction
    2. Love stories 3. Large type books
    I. Title
    823.9'2 [F]

    ISBN 978–1–84617–644–9

Published by
F. A. Thorpe (Publishing)
Anstey, Leicestershire

Set by Words & Graphics Ltd.
Anstey, Leicestershire
Printed and bound in Great Britain by
T. J. International Ltd., Padstow, Cornwall

This book is printed on acid-free paper

1

'A theatre?' Llinos Elliot gazed at her aunt in dismay. 'But I don't know anything about theatres!'

'It's not as if you'd be on stage performing, my dear,' Hannah Williams replied with a faint smile. 'The advertisement is for an administrator. Office work, that's what you are good at. One office can't be that different from another, surely.'

'I suppose not,' Llinos replied, dubiously, reaching out to take the copy of the local paper from Aunt Hannah's hand.

'Nothing ventured, nothing gained.'

Hannah smiled. Llinos knew her aunt was only trying to help. After all she had done, taking her in, with no questions asked as to why Llinos had left her job and her flat in such a hurry, to exchange the bright lights of London

1

for a small, seaside town along the North Wales coast, she didn't want to hurt her aunt's feelings. Besides, the woman at the temp agency she had signed on with that morning had been friendly and helpful, but also honest enough to warn her that she might have to travel quite a distance each time, and that in such a rural area she was unlikely to find the continuous supply of work she could have expected in London. Llinos couldn't afford to turn down any chance of a job, however small.

She smoothed the paper on the table in front of her and began to read the encircled advertisement.

Mabinogion Theatre, it began, **The Theatre on the Pier**.

The Theatre on the Pier. That jogged a memory somewhere, a memory from childhood, when her parents were still alive and they used to come each summer to visit Aunt Hannah during the school holidays. Llaneilwyn Pier was a rickety, old Victorian thing from when the little town had been a fashionable watering place.

Gladstone had visited it once, on his trip to Penmaenmawr, along the coast towards Llandudno, and that touch of glamour had kept the pier in reasonable repair when many others had been left to rot into the sea. The long, metal structure, strung along the water line by seaweed and bits of rubbish, had always been a part of her skyline as she played on the beach, or swam out as far as she dared, though she never did go beyond the fluted towers at the end.

They used to go along the pier itself in the evenings, she remembered, along with the other families, to watch the fishermen sitting patiently in the sunset, or the waves splashing on the rocks on the headland. She could almost still smell the candyfloss, and the distant whiff of fresh chips, and felt the salt and the sunburn tighten the skin on her face as they moved between the jugglers, and the sellers of large, stringed bird puppets that swayed and danced with clumsy movements, much to the annoyance of the Punch and Judy man with the narrow, cross-looking face, who was always attempting to collect as many children for his next show as possible, and eyeing any rival with deep suspicion.

'The puppet theatre,' she exclaimed as she scanned quickly through the advertisement. 'The Theatre on the Pier! It's the puppet theatre!'

'I thought you might remember it. You used to love going there when you were little. It's changed quite a bit since, of course. They do more community theatre, working with schools and such, but it's still Miss Bronski running it, though she must be well past retirement age by now.'

She must be. Llinos remembered a small, wrinkled woman who had seemed to her impossibly old back then, welcoming them into a magical world of beautifully-painted marionettes. There was the princess with slightly moth-eaten, long golden hair, dressed in fading silk, beautifully embroidered round the collar, accompanied by her prince in uniform, covered in tarnished brocade trimmings.

Even as a child, Llinos had known they were very old and very precious. Miss Bronski belonged to a long line of performers. The stories were passed down with the carefully-carved wooden marionettes to delight new generations of children. Performers, she remembered hearing, would willingly work for the minimum of pay just to gain the experience of working at the Theatre on the Pier.

'But I know even less about puppets,' she objected.

'I can't see many experienced office workers who will,' Aunt Hannah replied. 'To be honest with you, that place has been chaotic for as long as I can remember. I imagine they must be pretty desperate for someone to organise them to be advertising at all. I'd say you have as good a chance as any, and, in any case, it's always worth a try.'

Llinos saw Hannah's eyes sharpen.

But it's so public, she wanted to say. People come from all over the country to see Miss Bronski's puppet plays. Of all places, it was the most likely where she could be found.

Llinos pulled herself together, fighting down the panic rising inside her. Maybe she should have told Hannah the real reason for leaving, instead of her vague murmurings about stress, and a change of career. Ever since her parents had been killed in a car crash when she was twelve, Aunt Hannah's house had been Llinos's home.

Despite knowing nothing about children, and loudly declaring for years she didn't want any, Hannah had taken her in and provided a loving and secure home until Llinos had passed her exams and moved to London to take up a promising career as a Personal Assistant in a large insurance company.

Aunt Hannah would believe her. She wouldn't think she was stupid, or crazy, and just imagining things, and she knew anyway there was something wrong, that there was something her niece wasn't telling her.

How could I have been so stupid, Llinos asked herself, for the hundredth time. Why hadn't she been able to see beneath Philip's charm straight away, and realised how unnaturally intense he was about everything? At first, the tall, tanned young music journalist she had met in the sandwich bar, where she went regularly to buy lunch, had been easy company, funny, and interested in everything she did.

It had been so flattering after the humiliating break-up with Robin, her boyfriend of the past two years, and so much easier to pass him in the street, arms entwined around his own very young, very pretty, and extremely ambitious PA — the little matter Robin had omitted to inform her of for the last few months Llinos had been sharing his smart little house in Twickenham.

For a while, Philip had seemed like a breath of fresh air. At weekends, he drove her out into the countryside, to quaint, old-fashioned hotels, just the kind she adored. They had been for midnight swims, and moonlit walks on the beach, and drunk champagne as they watched the dawn mist rise over the ancient stone circle at Avebury. By the time bouquets of flowers began arriving each morning at her desk, he had all the other women in her office under his spell as well.

'How romantic!' her friend, Julia, had remarked, with a wishful sigh, at a large bunch of tightly-curled yellow roses. 'You don't get many men who do that kind of thing nowadays.'

'No,' Llinos had murmured, feeling mean, and ungrateful for her extraordinary luck, at her growing sense of her life being taken over and no longer her own.

'Do you like our time together?' Philip had demanded at her first attempt to take a step back from him.

'Of course I do.'

She was trying to be kind, to let him

down gently while sparing his feelings as much as possible. After everything they had shared, she felt, she owed him at least that.

'I love everything we do. No-one has ever taken me to such wonderful places before. It's just I need a little time on my own, now and again.'

She had smiled, trying to lighten the suddenly strained atmosphere.

'You know, darling, to wash my hair, do my nails, boast how lucky I am to my girl friends, that sort of thing.'

'You've never needed to before,' he answered, and she had never heard that tone in his voice before — petulant, like a child deprived of a puppy for adult reasoning that, to him, made no sense at all.

'Well, I do now,' she had retorted, sharper than she had intended, anger threatening to take over her carefully-considered tact.

'As you wish.'

She should have been relieved at his shrug and his lack of any further argument, but instead, she caught the cold stare of his pale blue eyes that watched her for the rest of their meal with a detached scrutiny.

After that, the magic had gone. He had called for her a few weeks later, attentive as ever, as if nothing had happened, but Llinos found she could no longer trust him. He was, she suddenly noticed, the one who always made the decisions about where they went and what they did. He took her to places he knew would please her, but always on his terms.

He wouldn't even let her pay for a drink, or a paper, as if she were dependant on him for everything, instead of a young woman with a bright career ahead of her who had always paid her own way. And it was always just the two of them. He never showed any interest in her family, or in getting to know her friends. Llinos found herself wishing for more and more days away from him.

Her colleagues in the office found it a

tragedy when she finally picked up the courage to finish with him. Llinos tried to look suitably sad, but inside she felt nothing but relief. At first, that is, for within days, she dreaded stepping outside the office, while going home was a nightmare.

'He's just always there,' she said, when she found the courage to explain to Julia at last, and as she had expected, Julia was sceptical.

'You're just getting paranoid, Llinos. You're bound to be in the same places sometimes.'

'It's not like that. He never comes up and says hello. He just watches. It's as if he wants me to know he's there.'

'Well, I've never noticed him when we've gone out to lunch together.'

'He doesn't do it when I'm with someone, at least not so obviously.'

'Llinos, are you quite sure about this?'

Julia finally seemed to be taking her seriously, concern in her eyes.

'Oh, yes, quite sure. It's been going

on for months now. I've even been to the police.'

'Llinos!'

That seemed to shake Julia. She had looked at her friend with real alarm.

'Did they do anything?'

'They tried to. They were very kind, and very sympathetic, and took it all very seriously. I was worried at first they'd think I was, well, some kind of nutcase.'

'Oh,' Julia had mumbled, blushing a little. 'So they've warned him off?'

'Not exactly.' Llinos had shivered, cold running right through her. 'You see, when they got to his flat, it was empty. I had no idea it was only rented. Anyhow, the landlord had no idea where he had gone. He'd just vanished, and all his personal stuff, too.'

'But they must have been able to get hold of him at work.'

'That was when I really began to get the jitters. You see, they'd never heard of him at the magazine. He'd never worked for them at all, and the references he'd given for the flat were all false. It was almost like he never existed at all.'

'That is spooky, Llinos!' Julia stared at her in dismay. 'What a horrible thing to happen. And now he's following you.'

'And no-one can do anything about it.'

'And how long has this been going on?'

'Six months,' Llinos whispered, fighting back the tears she had managed to keep at bay for so long.

Julia enveloped her friend in a warm hug, and when she let her go her eyes were sharp.

'But he's never actually done anything in all that time?'

'No.'

'In that case, Llinos, he's either just some sad idiot who can't let go, or he's done this before and he knows exactly what he can get away with.'

That was the moment a cold wind seemed to hurtle through Llinos, leaving her shaking, and unable to get warm for days. Ever since the word stalking had first been voiced by the very sympathetic policewoman, and Llinos began looking at every web-site she could find on the subject, the thought that Philip knew just how much he could get away with had been lurking uneasily at the back of her mind.

At Julia's words, she had felt suddenly certain. Philip knew so well how to manipulate people. He'd always managed to work his way into exactly the room he wanted at each hotel, whether they were booked up or not. He'd always managed to worm out of her her likes and dislikes without her even knowing he was doing it.

After Robin, and the bombshell of just how personal his personal assistant had become, Llinos had thought she had reached the lowest point of her self-esteem, but the thought that maybe Philip had never loved her for herself, only for some fantasy of her, which had nothing to do with the reality of her at all, had been almost too much.

That was the moment she'd known she had no choice but to leave. She could not bear to see him and be reminded of her blindness, and besides, if Julia was right, he could follow her like this for years, making her life a misery with nothing anyone could do.

Julia had been wonderful, backing up her story of leaving to look after a sick relative, and dealing with the letting of her flat, and acting as go-between for all the necessary correspondence, so that Llinos could just disappear, thankful that she had taken so little from Robin's house in her fury. Most of her possessions could fit into her car.

'So? What do you think, then?' Aunt Hannah asked, bringing Llinos back to the present, and the advertisement in her hand.

Llinos frowned. Damn Philip and his silly mind games! She'd lived for nearly a year looking over her shoulder every time she went out. Well, Philip was far away, and even if he did come looking for her then there would be no mistake that this was stalking, and the police would take it very seriously indeed. She wasn't going to have him rule her life any more. The puppet theatre sounded fun, and a complete change, which was just what she wanted, and who knew what it might lead to?

'It's certainly worth a try,' she replied, with a smile.

2

'Excuse me,' Llinos said as she tried once more to make her way through the crowd thronging the narrow walkway down the centre of the pier. It was a clear, brilliant April morning.

'What's your hurry, then?' a scornful voice demanded.

Llinos looked up to find herself squashed up against the Punch and Judy man glaring at her from the side of his brightly-coloured booth. He was the same Punch and Judy man as she remembered, hair whiter, and a good deal more wizened, but with the same undisguised dislike of anyone passing him by.

'I'm sorry. I'm trying to get to the theatre.'

'Oh, that. Blasted nuisance, that's what that is.'

Llinos blinked, smiled politely, and

made to push on, but the Punch and Judy man was there before her, stepping right into her path.

'Oi, you, Griffiths!' he shouted to a tall man in a pale linen jacket over a pair of faded jeans just ahead of them. 'I thought you said this would all be over by two o'clock.'

The man turned, revealing a darkly handsome face, jet-black hair, and grey eyes set in a decidedly flinty expression.

'We said we hoped to be finished by two if you remember, John. You know these things always over-run.'

'Well, I've got a business to run. I don't get grants and nice cosy sponsor-ship deals.'

The strong jawline hardened, but his opponent's tone remained deter-minedly courteous.

'I'm sure all the children taking part will be delighted to relax afterwards and watch your next performance, John,' he replied. 'Now if you'll excuse me, I've an urgent appointment to get to as soon as this is over.'

The Punch and Judy man muttered a comment Llinos felt it was better not to hear, and retreated to rearrange Mr Punch, strung up with a bunch of sausages and a collection of cotton bags that looked as if they contained the rest of the cast, just behind his booth.

Llinos began to push her way through again, but this time was brought to a stop by the sound of drums, and the infectious melody of a steel band. Thank goodness she had arrived here early, though at this rate she would still be late for her interview.

'Excuse me,' she began to the woman just in front of her, but the woman didn't hear, and when she looked at her, Llinos discovered tears rolling down her round cheeks. 'Are you all right?' she added, hastily.

'Isn't it wonderful?'

The woman turned to her, round face beaming, the tears still flowing. Llinos turned to the centre of the pier. A small procession was making its way down in a slow dance to the rhythm of the band. Through the people in front of her, Llinos could make out brightly-dressed adults accompanying a group of children, several of them in wheel-chairs, each carrying a small dragon high on a bamboo cane above their heads. The little dragons, in a colourful mixture of blues, greens, oranges, and glinting with gold paint, swayed and danced against the blue sky.

'They're lovely,' Llinos said, discovering her own feet were tapping as if wishing to join the rest of those around her, many of whom were already dancing away. 'It's just like a carnival.'

Things had changed. She never remembered anything like this from when she was little.

'They made them all themselves, you know. And this one, too.'

Slowly advancing towards them came a huge structure of a dragon, head supported on a pole moving slowly from side to side, while its enormous wings flapped above the heads of the crowd.

'There he is,' her neighbour practically squeaked with excitement. 'The wing nearest us. He looks so proud.'

The crowd had opened up in front of them and Llinos discovered a boy moving slowly along in a motorised wheel-chair. His head lolled uncontrollably from side to side, and his hands wavered around the pole, which was supported mainly by the chair itself, and a dark-haired young woman, who was bending and laughing with the boy, and then raising the pole up high to lift the wing up towards the sky.

The helper caught sight of the two of them watching, and bent down again to say something to the boy in the wheel-chair. He turned, face lit up with a broad smile, as he waved his free hand.

'He helped with the big dragon,' the woman said, waving back furiously. 'This had meant so much to Alex, being able to join in with this, just like the other children. When he was little, they said he'd never be able to do anything, and now he's part of the Theatre on the Pier.'

She began wiping her eyes with her sleeve.

'Oh, dear, you must think I'm quite mad,' she added, with an apologetic laugh.

'Oh, not at all,' Llinos replied quietly. 'I'd feel just the same.'

She watched as the little procession made its way towards the park on the shore, and all of a sudden this was not just a matter of getting a job to pay her way with Aunt Hannah, and be able to rent a flat of her own. Working with the Theatre on the Pier would never be just a job. It would be a passion, and a source of fulfilment. Instantly her stomach was all butterflies, her throat was dry, and her mind a blank, and she knew she wanted this job more than anything in her life.

Across the tail end of the procession, she saw the grey-eyed man of earlier watching her with a cool scrutiny. Of course! From what the Punch and Judy man had said, he must be a part of the theatre. Back to reality with a bump, Llinos looked at her watch. She was late, and he had spotted her dawdling, watching the procession instead of hurrying to be on time.

Well, it showed interest in their work, she tried to comfort herself as she pushed her way through the crowd. It was also, she had to admit, not exactly a professional start for an organiser and administrator. With her heart thumping louder than the distant band, Llinos finally made it to the theatre door.

* * *

'Well? How did it go?' Aunt Hannah asked as her niece came in through the door that evening.

Llinos groaned.

'Terrible. Awful. The pits. They must have thought I was a right idiot.'

'I'm sure it wasn't that bad.'

'Yes, it was. They asked me questions about making grant applications, and

23

the rôle of theatre in the community. I hadn't got a clue.'

'Those things you can learn, and you have plenty of other skills they can use. The main thing is if they liked you.'

Llinos sighed.

'I wouldn't bet on it. Oh, why did I think Armani was the thing to wear? I was totally out of place, and as for the shoes.' She kicked them off impatiently. 'You should have seen me tottering between all the dust and the bits of scenery like some overdressed call girl.'

Hannah suppressed a grin.

'I'm sure they didn't see you like that at all.'

'Oh, I'm sure they did, or at least that I hadn't the foggiest idea of what the job was about. Miss Bronski was nice. She could see I was really nervous and she did her best to put me at my ease.'

'There you are then. You'll have someone on your side when they make their decision.'

'Except that she's stepping down next Christmas and her nephew is taking over, and I don't think he liked me at all.'

She should have given up and not worried about it the moment she saw the stern grey eyes of the man on the pier watching her from behind the desk. Sara Bronski's nephew might have been impressed by the fact that she was late because she was watching the parade. But somehow she wouldn't bet on it.

'Is he now?' Aunt Hannah's eyebrows were raised. 'Well, and that's a boost. Adam Griffiths has directed plays in the West End, as well as working with community theatres in London and New York. He can be a bit of a perfectionist, I've heard.'

'So I gathered,' Llinos said, gloomily.

'I'm sure it went better than you think, and anyhow, if nothing comes of it, it's their loss, and it helped you brush up on your interview technique.'

'I suppose so,' Llinos replied.

Mr-stern-grey-eyes-hotshot theatre director or not, she still wanted this job badly.

'Well, if nothing else, at least it's got the colour back in your cheeks. I haven't seen you this glowing since you came back.'

That was true, Llinos realised. She hadn't looked in a mirror to see the glow, but she hadn't thought once about Philip all day, not even to look over her shoulder as she came back to the house, just in case. She was exhausted, but every little bit of her was tingling and alive.

Aunt Hannah was right. She may not get this job, but at least it had got her started in the right direction, and with the next one, she would make sure she did so much research she knew more about her prospective employers than they did, and nothing, but nothing would stop her from being on time.

She had just had a bath, and they were settling down with a relaxing glass of wine for a night in front of the telly in the interests of recovering from the day, when the phone rang. Llinos yawned as Aunt Hannah answered it.

After all those nerves, she was so tired that even a few sips of wine had gone straight to her head and she was feeling very sleepy. She closed her eyes, and was just drifting off when she heard Hannah's voice calling her.

'Mm?'

'It's for you, Llinos.'

That had her wide-awake in an instant. Had Philip found her already? Or maybe it was Julia, saying he was on his way. She gazed anxiously at her aunt, but Hannah was smiling broadly.

'Go on, quickly. It's Miss Bronski from the Theatre on the Pier. They've been trying to reach you on the mobile for ages.'

'I must have left it upstairs,' Llinos mumbled stupidly, too dazed to take in anything else.

'Hurry up. There's only one reason they'd be phoning you now. Get your skates on before they change their mind.'

Llinos felt her mouth drop open. They couldn't, not after that interview. She stumbled to the phone.

'Good evening, Miss Elliot.'

Sara Bronski's voice was reassuringly calm. The voice of someone who knows what they are doing.

'Good evening,' Llinos replied, hoping the wild racing of her heart could not be heard at the other end of the line.

'I'm sorry to phone so late. But I wanted you to know a letter will be with you tomorrow morning. We just thought you'd like to know that the interviewing panel have come to a decision, and we'd like to offer you the job of Administrator with the Theatre on the Pier.'

She must have misheard.

'Me? You're sure?'

'Quite sure.' The voice was dry, but amused.

'But I was awful, and I don't know anything about community theatres.'

'You'll pick that part up easily. You were very impressive, Miss Elliot. An outstanding candidate, in fact, and we're definitely in need of your other skills, unless, of course, you've changed your mind.'

That woke her up.

'No! Definitely not. I'd love to work for the Theatre on the Pier. I just can't quite believe it, that's all.'

'Oh, you will once you start, Llinos,' the reply came with a wry chuckle. 'Once you see the state of the place you'll believe it all right. You'll probably be cursing us all day.'

'I don't care,' Llinos said eagerly. 'I'm quite sure I'll love every minute of it.'

'I'm glad. We'll have to take up references, of course, and we like to have all our staff properly police checked, even those who don't have that much direct contact with the children, but that will all be just a formality, I'm quite sure. Have a restful weekend, and I'll phone you on Monday to arrange a day for you to come in and inspect us properly.'

'Thank you,' Llinos said. 'Thank you so much.'

She walked back slowly to the living-room where Hannah was waiting with an expectant smile.

'Well? Did you get it?'

Llinos nodded.

'Clever girl! I knew you would. Miss Bronski knows a good thing when she sees one. I'm sure you're going to love it there.'

'I know I will, Auntie.'

It was now sinking into Llinos's addled brain. This was real. She had a job. It may be a fraction of the salary she had been getting in London, but this was a job that would give her enough to rent a flat and start her life again, and give her a real sense of doing something worthwhile, something that would enable her to put Philip and his unhealthy obsession with her behind her, once and for all. At last it seemed she could move on with her life, and look towards a brighter future.

Aunt Hannah filled up their glasses.

'To the Theatre on the Pier,' she said, 'and all who work in her.'

'The Theatre on the Pier.' Llinos smiled.

3

Llinos stepped hesitantly through the open doors of the Theatre on the Pier. The entrance consisted of a little booking office, and a seating area with chairs and comfortable sofas, the walls brightened by an exhibition of set and costume designs for *A Midsummer's Night's Dream* made by local school-children.

Mrs Jones had shown her the exhibition when Llinos had come for her interview. It was part of the theatre's projects in local schools, she had explained, and it showed just how marvellously inventive children could be. Still full of the parade of giant puppets down the pier, and the delight on the face of the boy in the wheel-chair, Llinos had readily agreed.

She would have liked to look at it again now, but she had no intention of being late this time. Mrs Jones' nephew of the grey eyes would definitely not be impressed by a repeat of her tardiness at turning up for her interview, and since he was about to take over the running of the theatre, and would therefore be her boss, the last thing she could afford to do was to annoy him. There was, however, no-one to be seen.

Llinos hesitated. She had been in such a daze when Mrs Jones led her through the theatre to the little office at the back for her interview she had only the vaguest idea of the layout of the little puppet theatre. To one side of the booking office, she spotted a large-door, which, she seemed to remember, led into the auditorium.

The theatre was so compact they had crossed the stage on the way to the office, she remembered, along with the embarrassing recollection of tottering along in the impossibly high heels of her flimsy designer shoes. Well, at least she had taken the precaution of wearing loose cotton trousers and the most practical shoes she had brought with her in her rush to get away from London. She took a deep breath, and pushed her way through the door.

Inside, it was dark, with just a few lights glowing to reveal the steep bank of seats, and the small stage.

'Hello,' she called, experimentally, her voice echoing away into the darkness.

There was no reply. As her eyes adjusted to the gloom, she could make out a row of masks lined up on the stage, as if waiting for bodies to attach themselves at any moment, along with a large bird, that looked as if it might be an owl made of papiér maché, with newspaper still showing through a thin layer of white paint.

'Hello,' she tried again.

In the distance, a door banged, letting out a stream of furious argument taking place somewhere behind the stage.

'I don't damn well care,' a man's voice was saying. 'This is supposed to be an ensemble, Cerys, not a solo performance.'

The voices were coming nearer. It seemed she was about to meet the performers at last. Llinos braced herself.

'I didn't say it was a solo,' a female voice replied, sullenly.

'You didn't have to say anything,' the man retorted. 'It's the way you take over when it suits you.'

'I do not! I never do. You tell him, Mari. He's the one with the problem.'

'Oh, no, I'm staying out of this,' a third voice came, warm with humour.

Three figures made their way on to the stage, carrying mugs and a large packet of biscuits as if about to settle down for a picnic. Llinos didn't know exactly what she had expected, but the three were all very young, and dressed in ancient, loose-fitting clothes that were covered in more than their fair share of paint.

They had the appearance more of decorators than performers, apart from the fair-haired young woman in the centre, who was tall and willowy, with a strikingly beautiful face that would draw all eyes whether she tried to hog the spotlight or not.

'Hello,' Llinos called, before the argument could continue, and had the embarrassment of all three of them stopping in their tracks to look down at her as she stood below the stage. 'I'm Llinos. Llinos Elliot, the new administrator. Mrs Jones asked me to come in today to look around and to meet everyone. I wasn't quite sure which was the best way in.'

'Oh, hi. Come on in,' a dark-haired young woman said, who Llinos recognised as the owner of the humorous voice, and the helper of the boy in the wheel-chair from the day of her interview. 'You're all right. This is the only way through to the back. It's all rather cramped, I'm afraid.'

Her smile was bright and friendly.

'I'm Mari Lewis. This is Rhys Owen.' She gestured towards a lanky young man with short, spiky bleached hair and a shy grin.

'Hi, Llinos. Come to keep us in order then?' he remarked.

'Only the office,' Llinos replied and his grin broadened.

'Wait till you see it first.'

'Take no notice of Rhys's little jokes,' Mari said. 'We don't want to put you off before you start. And this is Cerys.'

'Hello,' the fair-haired girl said.

From the expression in her large blue eyes, it seemed she regarded any office worker as a definitely lower order of existence.

'Our prima donna,' Rhys put in, as if he couldn't quite resist the opportunity for the jibe.

'Don't be stupid,' Cerys snapped.

A sense of humour was not, it seemed, counted amongst her talents.

'Mrs Jones is around somewhere,' Mari said. 'They're trying to sort out the design for the posters for our Christmas show.' She grinned. 'She hates that sort of thing. She'll be so glad to be able to hand all that over.'

'Is that what you are working on now?' Llinos asked.

'Yes. We always do a story from the old Welsh stories of the Mabinogion for Christmas. It's a sort of tradition as the Mabinogion is the official name of the theatre, although everyone just calls it the Theatre on the Pier. This year we're doing a mixture of masks and puppets to tell the story of Blodeuwydd, the woman made from flowers who tried to kill her husband to be with her lover and was turned into an owl. And Cerys, of course, is playing Blodeuwydd.'

Cerys looked smug at this, apparently deaf to the dryness in Mari's tone.

'Which means at last she can murder me,' Rhys remarked.

Cerys scowled, and seemed about to make some scathing reply, when her eyes focussed over Llinos's shoulder at something, or rather someone, making their way through the darkness of the auditorium. In a transformation as miraculous as any she might make in her rôle as the woman made out of flowers, Cerys somehow became even more slender and willowy than before, as if she were a fragile little thing Rhys could reduce to tears at any moment with his heartlessness. She turned her head and gazed at him with a resigned patience that would almost certainly have irritated a saint.

'At least you get brought back to life again,' she murmured. 'I have to wander the earth as an ugly little owl for the rest of my existence.'

'Personally, I rather like owls,' Rhys returned, sweetly.

But Cerys was no longer aware that he even existed.

Her eyes followed the tall form of Adam Griffiths as he made his way towards them as if there was only one man alive in the entire universe.

'Llinos has arrived, Adam,' Mari called. 'Sara is tied up with the printers. Can you show her around?'

'You're early.'

The cool eyes scrutinised Llinos. He

didn't seem exactly overjoyed to see her, she realised with a sinking feeling. Maybe he hadn't wanted to offer her the job at all, and had been overruled by his aunt.

'I was trying to make up for being late last time,' Llinos replied, with a feeble attempt at a smile.

'Oh, that was our fault. Slight technical hitch with the dragon at the last moment,' Mari put in, quickly. 'We were terribly late with the parade. No wonder you couldn't get through.'

He grunted, as if unconvinced.

'If you'd like to follow me, Miss Elliot.'

Out of the corner of her eye, Llinos caught Cerys frowning at them, as if she suspected they were setting out to get up to all sorts back stage.

'We've nearly worked out all the Blodeuwydd story, Adam,' she called, loudly.

'Good,' he replied. 'We can discuss it later.'

'We're just not sure about the

transformation of the flowers into Blodeuwydd,' she persisted. 'I'm sure you can think of a much better way.'

'Adam's got enough on his plate,' Rhys said, frowning. 'Anyhow, Cerys, that's our job. Leave Adam out of it.'

'Children, children!'

It was Mari, laughing, but with a serious edge to her voice.

'Take no notice, Llinos, you'll get used to them. They like each other really. I'm sure we'll end up being bridesmaids at their wedding one day.'

'Over my dead body,' Rhys snorted.

'As if,' Cerys added, with scorn.

Llinos sent a quick glance towards Adam Griffiths, not quite sure what he was making of this. Cerys had been sending such clear signals he might not take kindly even to a joke that she might be interested in anyone else. To her surprise, she found he was smiling. He had turned his face away from the stage to hide his amusement from Cerys, which unfortunately meant Llinos got the full brunt of it.

Unfortunate, because Adam Griffiths' smile transformed his face. It was a mobile, humorous face, she discovered to her alarm. Even those grey eyes of his glowed warm and surprisingly gentle.

After all, it turned out to be the kind of face that could get a girl into all kinds of difficulties, if she let it, of course, which she wouldn't, because she barely knew him. She wasn't about to make that kind of mistake again.

Llinos dragged her eyes away, and fixed them on Cerys's expression of ethereal beauty. How on earth could she compete with that, she scolded herself, severely.

'I'll show you the office first,' she found he was saying, his face still softened by his laughter, 'if you promise not to run away the moment you see it.'

Llinos found herself smiling, even though she'd decided it was probably safer not to show any unnecessary friendliness at all.

'Everyone seems to think this office is a horror story,' she replied. 'It's making me nervous.'

'Ah, well, wait until you see it,' he returned.

4

Well, it might not exactly be a horror story, but it was pretty bad. Files lay piled everywhere, in great heaps on the floor, and almost completely covering the desk, leaving only room for a rather ancient-looking computer and a very dead plant.

Files and boxes lay so high and so thick in front of the window that no-one had been able to reach it to clean it, leaving the glass covered in a layer of grime.

'I'm afraid my aunt has been so busy just keeping this place going all this has been neglected,' Adam said, apologetically. 'She knows where everything important is, and can lay her hands on it in a moment, but it means no-one else can, and she is not as young as she was, and if anything happened . . . Besides, it doesn't give the right impression. We can't keep meeting grant officers and the like on the stage. They might start to get suspicious that we have a secret money-printing business back here.'

He gave a rueful smile.

'I know it's a lot to ask of anyone, Llinos, and the salary isn't exactly generous, but we were lucky to get what we did from the local authority to fund this post. We'll all quite understand if you feel you've been taken on under false pretences.'

Llinos eyed him closely. He was giving her a way out, but he was also giving himself an opportunity for getting rid of her, which, if he didn't want her in the first place, might be exactly his idea. Come to think of it, maybe his aunt wasn't detained elsewhere after all. Maybe he had manipulated things to work out this way so he could have this opportunity.

She gave herself a mental shake. She had become so suspicious since Philip, questioning everyone's motives, trusting no-one. She couldn't spend her whole life thinking everyone was like Philip. She had learned a valuable lesson in being careful, and more wary in future, but to be consumed with suspicion would box her into a corner, just as surely as Philip had tried to do.

'I rather like the idea of a challenge,' she said aloud.

'Really?'

If he was disappointed, or relieved, it was impossible to say, but his eyes were watching her again, back to their former coolness.

'I had better show you back stage, then,' he said. 'Much of that will eventually need sorting out as well. We've collected so much stuff over the years and I'm sure much of it can go. I'm going to have to be more ruthless than my aunt, I'm afraid. We simply don't have the space to develop new things any more. It was designed as purely a puppet theatre using mario-nettes. That's our main problem, as we're hard pressed to find the space for the large structures like the dragon that we make with the kids.'

He relaxed again into a smile.

'I'm told that traditionally large puppets like that are burned once they've served their purpose, but it seems a pity after all that hard work. I expect I'll turn out just as reluctant as my aunt to throw anything away, and we won't be able to move for rubbish.'

'It can't be that bad, surely.'

'You can still say that after seeing the office?' he demanded and Llinos laughed.

'I think you'd better just show me,' she said.

The storeroom was not much bigger than the office, and just as crammed and dusty, but Llinos gazed around her, enchanted. It was like walking into all her childhood stories at once.

Pieces of miniature scenery were stacked around the walls, some at quite precarious angles. A beanstalk hung from the ceiling, next to the round towers of a fairy-tale castle, and the remains of a pirate ship, along with forests of trees made from cardboard, and delicate sea-life created from some kind of transparent film that fluttered with an iridescent hue as they passed.

'Impressive, eh?' Adam said.

'Beautiful,' she replied, making her way over boxes of tissue paper, past a large head of a Chinese dragon stacked amongst three outsized swans and a mermaid taller than herself, constructed out of an intricate network of willow, and half covered in tissue.

'She will be a giant lantern for the Christmas parade,' he explained. 'She should have candles inside her, but Health and Safety would have a fit, so it'll be battery-operated torches instead. You can see the glow through the tissue paper. It looks spectacular, and the children love them.'

'Do the children in the wheel-chairs join in with that, too?'

'Oh, yes. They're from the special needs units from several of the local schools. We have sessions for them once a week, making giant lanterns like these. They take a long time, so we start getting ready for Christmas as soon as the summer holidays are over.'

'It makes me wish I was creative like that,' Llinos said.

'Don't worry, I'm sure you'll have your chance to try. I'm quite sure you'll be roped in at some point,' he replied with a smile. 'There's always a last-minute panic when everyone is working all night to get the things finished in time. I'm sure you'll be very good. Catrin said you really seemed to have a feel for the giant puppets.'

'Catrin?' She looked at him, puzzled.

'Alex's mum. The boy in the wheel-chair holding the dragon's wing in the parade when you came for your interview. She said she spoke to you.'

'That's right. She was so proud of him she was in tears. It was really touching.' She frowned. 'How did she know I was being interviewed?'

'Well, let's say you weren't exactly planning to go fishing in that suit.'

Llinos felt herself blushing. She was never going to live down the Armani, she could see that, and she'd once been so proud she had been able to afford it, and those ridiculous shoes!

'Catrin's one of our most active trustees, and she works tirelessly for those special needs kids. She didn't have a say in your appointment as she wasn't on the interviewing panel, but she did drop large hints.'

He cleared his throat, a little embarrassed.

'I'm afraid she'd seen me looking at you, so I'd know exactly who she meant.'

'I know I was late,' she began, but she was brought up short by his smile.

'That wasn't why I was looking at you,' he said.

'Oh.'

There was no mistaking his tone, and this time she felt herself blush bright scarlet.

'I'm sorry, that was crass of me, although perhaps not as crass as also wondering if you'd stopped next to her on purpose, knowing she was a trustee. It might have helped your cause no end to start buttering her up with a show of interest in her little boy, you know.'

'What?' she said furiously.

'It happens. The job market is a cut-throat one these days.'

'Not for the kind of money you're offering!' she snapped.

He at least had the grace to wince at this.

'Touché.'

'I'm sorry, I didn't mean to be rude.'

'Well, then, you should have been,' he returned, graciously. 'I would have deserved it.'

'I've worked for lots of money for years. As long as I have enough to get by, I'd much rather live on less and do something I can really believe in,' she said.

'I know. That's what stood out at your interview. The other two we saw were clearly seeing this just as a stepping-stone to something better.

With your business background, I wasn't entirely convinced at the time, but Catrin was quite right. You have a real feel for what we are doing.'

He held out his hand.

'Friends?'

'Friends,' she replied.

His grip was firm, but warm.

'Good. Now that's settled, I can take you out for a coffee.'

He saw her hesitate.

'Strictly as business,' he added. 'I, for one, am not going to discuss your future duties amongst all this dust and chaos. Besides, it might frighten you into running away. We can get an excellent cappuccino in the café on the pier, and some fresh air after all this lot.'

The wariness was still in her eyes, he noted. At the interview he had taken it as a sign she had something to hide, something like showing an exaggerated sympathy for a trustees' son to buy her support. Adam frowned. It came of being in the competitive business of commercial theatre for too long, making him suspicious that everyone he met was on the make, and prepared to use any means to get to the top.

He didn't believe that of Llinos, not any more. In fact, he noted to himself wryly, if he'd any inkling his prospective new employee was just as attractive on the inside as she was in her appearance, he might have not taken her on at all. Dating colleagues always ended in tears, in his experience. Maybe that was the root of her suspicion, too.

'I haven't made a move on an employee for years,' he remarked, lightly, repositioning the mermaid, as if afraid she might fall over. 'I have rules about that sort of thing.'

'So do I,' Llinos replied firmly, almost convincing herself that her feeling was one of relief that this was clear between them.

She had no intention of any involvement at all with any man, however attractive, not for a long time.

'Good. Now we've established the

casting couch is closed, perhaps we can go for that coffee after all.'

He could be very charming when he put his mind to it. But she had learned her lesson. She was not about to fall for charming again. The faster Cerys worked her many attractions into his notice the better, as far as Llinos was concerned, and she would make sure she stayed out of his way as much as she could. But one cup of coffee could do no harm.

'Coffee sounds like an excellent idea,' she said.

5

For the next few weeks, Llinos found herself working harder than she had ever worked before, not that she minded. It was just the kind of absorbing, satisfying work she needed to free her mind from the memories of those last months in London, dreading her next sighting of Philip in the crowd.

Besides, hard work was also a good way of keeping thoughts of Adam Griffiths from creeping into her mind, though this was a good deal harder, given that he had now fully taken over the running of the puppet theatre from his aunt.

She caught at least one glimpse of him most days, as he arranged the projects with children in the local schools, and oversaw the preparations for the Christmas performance and parade. And, somehow, despite their mutual agreement on not dating work colleagues, the coffees on the pier had remained a regular feature, for purposes of work only!

'Wow, you have made a difference. You can even see there's a floor in here,' Mari remarked one afternoon.

She came into the little office on a regular mission to collect orders for chocolate bars and the odd cake, for what she and Rhys termed as stress relief. Only Cerys ignored this ritual, with an air of virtue and a quick smoothing of her streamlined figure.

'I've thrown so much old filing away it's scary,' Llinos said, climbing down from the desk that she had pushed against the window to clean the filthy panes. 'There, that brings in more light.'

'I'm sure Adam wouldn't let you destroy anything that's of value.'

'Oh, no. And I make sure he has a look through the to-be-shredded pile before I get going.'

She patted the shiny new shredder

with affection. She had spent many a happy hour quietly feeding through old invoices and advertisements.

'And the new computer's arriving tomorrow.'

'Now that's a day I never thought to see. I was sure that ancient box would be here for ever. It's almost pre-mouse, that thing.'

She nodded to the sad-looking machine relegated to one corner, on its way to retirement after Llinos had made sure all the important data had been transferred.

'You'll have this place in regular working order by Christmas, you'll see.'

'With all the store room to clear out? Not a chance,' Llinos replied with a smile.

During the time she had worked at the puppet theatre, she and Mari had become friends. Mari had always been the one ready to answer questions, however busy she was rushing off to workshops, or working on the Christmas performance.

When Llinos had started to look around for a flat of her own to rent, feeling, despite Hannah's protests, that she had disturbed her aunt's peace quite enough, Mari had scoured every paper and newsagent for miles around, and found the small attic flat on the same row as her own was coming up for rent, even before it reached the papers.

Llinos had jumped at the chance, and loved every part of it. It had a living-room overlooking the sea, a compact kitchen and the bedroom with the skylight through which, on clear nights, she could see the stars as she fell asleep. She didn't mind that they were student flats, with so many crammed in one building. It was reassuring, knowing that she was surrounded by people.

She looked up to find Mari eyeing her.

'Sure you won't change your mind about tonight? You haven't been out since you started here. Come and let your hair down a little. It's only me,

Cerys and Rhys, and we aren't exactly going to paint the town red. You're doing me a favour. Save me from playing gooseberry to their squabbling all evening.'

Llinos laughed. Cerys might play all sweetness and light when Adam was nearby, but at all other times she couldn't resist rising crossly to Rhys's bait, even, Llinos was sure, during tonight's drink to celebrate his birthday. All of a sudden, she knew how she missed going out and meeting people.

She'd been shut in for so long when Philip was following her about in London, and when she first moved here, that she was growing used to spending long evenings on her own, reading or working her way through videos. The thought of being out amongst people just enjoying themselves in a normal way was too tempting.

'Well, maybe, but I mustn't be too late back.'

'Nor will we, don't worry. I wanted to

do this on Friday, but Rhys is going out with his mates from university, which is serious partying. So tonight is very genteel, with clear heads for the morning. What do you think?'

'Sounds good to me,' Llinos said with a smile.

The evening was unseasonably warm for early October, and the four found themselves a table outside the Prince's Arms Hotel, amongst the quiet groups of townsfolk and late tourists wandering along the sea front. It was all so peaceful that Llinos found herself relaxing, and forgetting her habit of scanning any crowd for a familiar face.

She was enjoying the sharp, cold taste of her lager, and the lights coming up all around, reflected in the gentle roll of water in the bay as the purple haze of evening darkened into night.

'Those giant lanterns you are making with the special needs kids look wonderful,' she said to Mari.

'Don't they? It was such a good idea of Adam's to take the theme of King

Arthur this year. Alex and the other boys have loved making Merlin and all the knights, and the girls are having such fun with the ladies.'

'I still don't get where the mermaid fits in,' Rhys said with a grin.

'The Lady of the Lake, of course.'

'She wasn't a mermaid!'

'She lived in water, didn't she? Anyhow, have you never heard of poetic license?'

'Those two have just been dying to make a mermaid ever since they started,' Rhys said, with a wink at Llinos. 'It's a girl thing. I'm sure they've still got their Little Mermaid dolls next to their beds.'

'Not that you'll ever find out,' Mari swiftly retorted.

'Now that is low,' Rhys replied, with an exaggerated show of being mortally wounded.

It was not the sort of thing that Cerys would normally let by her, either, but she was preserving an ominous silence and smiling sweetly into space, which,

Llinos recognised with a sinking in her stomach, could only mean one thing. Sure enough, the next moment a familiar figure loomed out of the crowd around them.

'I like the mermaid,' Adam said, leaning over to place a pint on the table in front of Rhys. 'I'm sure King Arthur, or at least his knights, could have no objections to mermaids. Happy birthday, Rhys.'

'Cheers, mate,' Rhys said.

'Can I get anyone else a drink?' Adam asked.

'I'm fine, thanks,' Mari replied with a smile.

'Me, too,' Llinos said.

'Cerys?' Adam asked, oblivious to her adoring look up at him.

'Just a tonic water, please.'

'Ice and lemon?'

'Yes, please, Adam. Thank you.'

'Well, and that's a first,' Mari said as Adam made his way to the crush at the bar. 'He doesn't usually join us after work. There must be a special attraction here tonight.'

Her look was pointed towards Llinos sitting next to her that even Cerys caught her meaning, and scowled.

'I'm sure he just came to get Rhys a birthday drink,' Llinos replied, trying to suppress the colour rising to her cheeks.

'Oh, you do, do you?' Mari returned, laughing. 'I don't think Rhys's company is that attractive, somehow.'

'Speak for yourself,' Rhys shot back, with a good-natured smile, as Mari reached out to the table behind them and deftly removed a spare chair to place between herself and Llinos.

'Beautiful evening,' Adam said, returning with the drinks and showing no objections to taking the place made for him. 'You never get it quite like this in London.'

'I used to like the city lights at night,' Llinos replied, 'but you're right, this is very special.'

She turned back to resume her conversation with Mari but somehow her friend had both their companions engaged in conversation, leaving Adam and Llinos to amuse each other. Adam grinned to himself. Mari was not being very subtle, but it was just a friendly drink after work, and he had no objections at all.

'The office is looking quite civilised at last,' he remarked.

'I've got another pile of stuff for you to look through, I'm afraid, and there's loads more stacked in the corners. I've been trying to clear some space for the new computer.'

'Well, it looks like a miracle to me, and to Aunt Sara. I don't know what we'd do without you.'

There was a faintly mischievous smile lurking round his lips.

'Pity, really, as it means I can't possibly sack you.'

'Sack Llinos!'

Having caught this, Rhys was all attention.

'Why on earth would you want to sack Llinos?'

'I don't, but on the other hand it could have its advantages.'

'Well, try it, and you'll have a riot on your hands.'

'Or three,' Mari put in, 'or perhaps two,' she added, catching the look on Cerys's face.

It was a well-known disadvantage of working with Adam Griffiths that he had a rule about never going out with any of his employees, and Cerys had the look of someone on whom the impossibility of his ever breaking this rule for the sake of her beauty was slowly dawning.

'I think I can safely promise not to sack Llinos,' Adam returned with a wry smile. 'She's just too good at her job. So come on then, Rhys,' he brightened, deliberately changing the subject. 'So just how old are you going to admit to being?'

Llinos joined in the good-humoured laughter as the subject of Rhys's age moved on to other subjects. She felt relaxed and happy, content for the moment just to have Adam sitting so close she could reach out and touch him, and with his smile turned towards her frequently to draw her into the easy flow of conversation.

At least this way, it suddenly struck her, she felt safe, free to get to know him better, without any possibility of him asking her out, so that one day, if there was ever a chance of things changing, she would be sure, absolutely sure.

She suddenly became aware of eyes watching her. She looked up to see Cerys watching her face, her mouth tight, her expression one of suppressed fury. Startled, Llinos did not know how to look away. She had no wish to make an enemy of Cerys, and certainly not with that amount of venom bottled up inside her!

The intensity was making her scalp tingle. Llinos blinked. In a moment, Cerys had bent forward, eyes glowing softly in response to some remark of Adam's.

As if in slow motion, Llinos saw her lip curve in a smile and open to begin her reply, but for Llinos, the words were as far away as if they had come from the other side of the world. Cerys had clearly forgotten her, or at least no longer had eyes for her. But the venom was still there, watching her, rooting her to the spot and scattering her wits to pieces.

What a fool she had been, Llinos thought suddenly. Of course Cerys was far too sure of her own charms to see her as any kind of serious rival for Adam's attentions.

There was another gaze from amongst the drinkers in the bar that had been observing every smile Adam had turned towards Llinos, and every smile she had returned — one that was still watching, and would never forgive either of them for any smallest, imagined piece of involvement between the two of them.

As if drawn, Llinos raised her eyes slowly to meet those of a man sitting at the table opposite, half hidden behind his newspaper. The eyes glinted at her for a moment, then disappeared completely behind the pages.

'I must go.'

She stood up suddenly, knocking her chair over in her haste.

'Llinos? Are you all right?'

Adam was on his feet in a moment, face filled with anxiety.

'I'm fine. I'm just tired. I really must go.'

They were all looking at her as if she had become a stranger, and the old panic began to rise within her.

'I'll walk you home,' Adam said.

'No!'

That was the last thing she needed, the last thing he should do!

'It's all right, really.'

'I'll come with you. I'm so tired I'm almost ready for bed myself,' Mari said quietly, standing up. 'Come on, Llinos, I'll even make you some hot cocoa if you're lucky.'

Llinos smiled at her gratefully. She turned back briefly towards the nearby table, but the man was no longer there, just his half-finished coffee standing on the table, and the newspaper, its pages moving slowly in the air.

'I would like that,' she murmured.

'Are you sure you don't want me to get you both a taxi?'

Adam was still frowning. He probably thought she had simply drunk too much, Llinos thought miserably. Wasn't that what city girls with designer suits and silly, strappy little sandals were supposed to do after work? He probably imagined she had got up to all sorts in London. He'd probably be demanding she took a drugs test every Monday from now on. Llinos shook her head.

'I'd prefer to walk,' she replied, swinging her bag over her shoulder.

Suddenly, all she wanted was to get out of here, to get back to her flat, and have time to think.

6

'Are you sure there is no way he could have found out where I am?' Llinos could hear her panic even in her own ears as she spoke.

'I'm sure,' Julia replied at the other end of the phone.

'He hasn't been to the office? There hasn't been any burglary in your flat, that sort of thing?'

'No, nothing. Llinos, are you sure it was him?'

'Yes, as sure as I can be. I couldn't make out his face, it was all so sudden, and he was too far away, but I know that look, Julia, I just know it.'

'Then go straight to the police.'

'And say what?'

Llinos fought back her tears, trying to keep calm and think clearly. Mari had been very kind and sweet when they arrived back just a few hours ago.

She made cocoa, just as she had promised, and chatted easily about her work with the children and didn't attempt any questions at all. Llinos had promised to go straight to bed, but the moment her new friend had left, the old fear was there, deep in her stomach again.

She had checked and double-checked every lock, every window, and even the skylight in her tiny bathroom. She had opened every wardrobe, and every cupboard and drawer, even the tiny ones not even a mouse could hide in. But still she could feel those eyes of his, watching her.

'Julia, what could I tell them? That I felt a stare from a man who can't possibly know where I am and whose face I couldn't even see properly, and who wasn't there when I tried to find him again? They'll think I'm nuts.'

'I'm sure they won't. They'll check with the police here in London, and they'll know all about you, and that you're not a crackpot. They take these things very seriously, remember, Llinos.'

'But maybe it wasn't him. No-one knows where I am apart from you, so how could he have found out? Maybe I really was just imagining it after all. I want to be sure, Julia, not be the woman who cried wolf.'

There was a moment's silence at the other end of the phone. Then she heard Julia sigh, as if admitting defeat.

'OK, OK. Look, I'll see what I can find out, check out everything I can think of.'

'Thanks, Julia, you're a star.'

'And you take care, hear me? I'm sure he's harmless, even if it is him, but don't take any chances, and call the police at the slightest thing.'

'Oh, don't worry, I will. No way am I going through all that again. And I've got my dad's old cricket bat under the bed for good measure!'

'Llinos!'

'Oh, I'm not expecting to use it,' Llinos replied.

Julia suddenly seemed very far away,

and she felt very alone.

'But he's never going to get the chance to rule my life again, not ever.'

★　★　★

Llinos arrived early for work next day, and made sure she was busy before any of the others arrived.

'Sure you're all right?' Mari asked.

'Oh, fine. I was just very tired, and it's so long since I've been out for a drink I'm not used to alcohol, that's all. I was falling asleep where I sat. I just needed to get to bed.'

'Well, if you're sure.'

She didn't seem entirely convinced, and Llinos smiled brightly.

'Everything's fine.'

'Because if you ever need anything, I'm here.'

'Thanks, Mari.'

Her friend's concern, however, seemed to be catching, and try as she might, Llinos could not relax that day, or the day after, for the rest of that week.

There was no sign of Philip, however hard she scanned the faces in the crowds, and however much she looked behind her as she rushed home after work.

The moment she shut the door in the flat she found herself checking the windows, opening cupboards and searching round for any sign of anything being moved or disturbed, but nothing ever was, however hard she looked. Maybe he hadn't been there at all, or maybe this was all part of a waiting game, to stretch her nerves to breaking point and wear her down.

If that was what he was after, he was succeeding, she realised by the end of the second week. Every muscle in her body was taut, even when she tried to sleep. She was alert at every creak of the boards in the flats around her, and every voice on the stairs. At work she was finding it increasingly hard to concentrate on anything. The smallest box seemed to weigh heavily in her arms, and she found herself misplacing papers she had sorted out just a moment before.

Maybe, she wondered to herself as she sat in the office and tried in vain to make sense of the inner workings of the new computer, the only solution would be to move again. But to where? And if Philip really had found her here, despite all her precautions, he could surely find her again. Besides, she didn't want to move, she realised suddenly. She loved her work at the theatre, and she had made good friends.

'Fancy a cappuccino?'

Llinos jumped as the one face she had been thinking of appeared at the door behind her. The cup of cold tea in her hand shot off, dispersing murky brown liquid all over a pile of newly-printed letters. She cursed aloud.

'Sorry, I didn't mean to startle you.'

He reached over for the kitchen roll perched on a shelf for just such emergencies and began to help her mop up the mess.

'I bet that's a morning's work I've just ruined.'

'It's OK, they're all saved on to the hard drive, if I can find them again,' she muttered to herself.

'One of those days, eh?'

His tone was light, but the grey eyes were back to the severe look. A knot tightened in Llinos's stomach. He must have noticed, like the rest of them, how her work had deteriorated over the past days. Perhaps the coffee was meant to be more than a mere social occasion. If he thought she'd lost interest in the job, well, that was all she needed.

'I'm sorry,' she began, miserably.

She felt tired, and ready to scream, and even more ready to find the nearest shoulder to cry on, and Adam's shoulder was temptingly solid, and temptingly near. She swallowed hard, and tried to pull herself back together again.

'Coffee,' he said, firmly, 'and no need to be sorry. Let's just get out of here.'

Without a moment for her to protest, he had clicked the computer into sleep mode, and was pulling her up, and through the door into the passageway towards the stage, and out to the front entrance.

'Well?' Adam prompted, as they sipped their coffee. 'So are you going to tell me what this is all about?'

'Oh, nothing. I've just been over-doing things, what with moving and everything. I'm sorry I've not been quite together at work.'

Out in the fresh air, she was feeling a little better. She wasn't going to let Philip ruin this for her, and she was going to fight to hang on to this job with all her might. She found Adam watching her with a frown.

'I'll be back to normal from now on, I promise.'

'Forget the work.' His tone was abrupt. 'I'm here to have my ear bent, Llinos. You haven't been yourself since the night we went out for Rhys's birthday. If there's something at the theatre that's bothering you . . . '

'No!' she replied anxiously. 'No, you

mustn't think that. I love working at the theatre. I'd hate to have to leave.'

'And why should you want to leave?'

He watched her chew her lip.

'None of us wants you to go. We all want to help. Has Cerys been saying things?'

'No. Cerys has been fine. She's left me alone.'

'Good. But I'm not going to leave it. I hate to see you distressed in this way. Llinos, has this anything to do with the reason you left London?'

His eyes were full of concern, and something else she didn't dare to even begin to think about. She was tired of running, of holding this inside her on her own. She had to begin trusting someone, and deep in her heart she knew for certain that the man before her was one she could trust, body and soul. She nodded, wordlessly.

'I thought it might. Rhys was worried about you this morning. He saw you come out of the police station on your way to work. He wasn't quite sure what to do about it, so I'm afraid he asked me. Is something seriously wrong?'

'Yes. Look, I haven't done anything to get in trouble with the law, or anything.'

'Hey, Llinos, this is me you're talking to. I hope I know you well enough to be quite certain it wasn't you who committed any crime, if that is what this is about.'

Llinos found herself smiling faintly. He reached across the table and took her hands in his. Relief flooded over her.

'I know.'

'So, are you going to tell me?'

'Yes.'

'Good.' He eyed her pale face. 'I don't know about you, but I could do with a stiff brandy, and don't worry about work. You're having the afternoon off, as of now.'

His eyes gave a brief twinkle as he rose to go to the bar.

'And we can deal with the gossip later.'

Llinos smiled to herself. At least from

now on she wouldn't be alone in this. Whatever Adam thought of her, at least he would know she was not drunk, or mad, when the uneasiness came over her and she began seeing Philip in the crowds. She shut her eyes, relaxing a little.

It had taken her hours to work up the courage to make her way down to the local police station earlier, and she had gone inside with her heart really and truly in her mouth. She needn't have worried. The police had been very sympathetic and taken her very seriously from the first moment.

Julia had been quite right about that. It didn't matter that she couldn't be sure it had been Philip watching her that evening of Rhys's birthday. They'd sent for all the details from London, and assured her that if she found anything to make her uneasy, however slight, they would take it very seriously. Thank goodness she had reported Philip in London!

In the bag at her feet, her mobile sent

out its little tune. For a moment she ignored it. She didn't want anyone to disturb this moment. The mobile continued, persistently. She'd forgotten to switch on the voice-mail, it seemed. Llinos reached into her bag and picked it up to switch the annoying jingle off. As she did so, her finger paused as she saw the name of her caller. Suddenly, she was tense again, and there was a bitter taste in her mouth.

'Julia?'

'Llinos. Thank goodness I caught you.'

From the moment she heard the barely-controlled wobble in her friend's voice, Llinos knew that every fear lurking in the back of her mind was no imagination at all.

'Julia, what is it?'

'Llinos, I never thought to check before . . . '

'What?' Llinos interrupted.

'It's just I've a day off today, and I was sorting through some of my stuff in my flat, and I came across my old address book.'

Llinos felt her blood run cold, and her scalp begin to prickle.

'And?'

'I don't know why I looked. I don't use it any more. I just keep it in case I lose the new one. I'm sorry, Llinos, nothing else was missing, so I never dreamed . . . '

'What? What was missing?'

'The page with your aunt's address in it. She's your next of kin and . . . '

'Are you sure you put it in there, not just in the new one?'

'Oh, yes, quite sure. And in any case, you can see where it has been ripped out. The entire page is missing.'

7

'It must have been him I saw that night when we went out for Rhys's birthday,' Llinos said, stacking files on the shelves back in the office as if her life depended on it. 'I should have known Philip wouldn't let it go so easily.'

'Well, at least you're not alone now, and the police were very helpful and efficient,' Adam replied.

'I know. Thanks for being so understanding, and for going back there with me,' she replied with a smile.

She didn't know how she would have got out of that café after the phone call from Julia, if Adam had not been there to listen to her garbled explanation about Philip, and her panic at Aunt Hannah's address being stolen from Julia's address book. He had made her drink a glass of brandy while they waited for a taxi to the police station.

'No problem. I just wish you'd told us before.'

'I thought maybe you'd think I was making it up, or it was me who had an obsession with him and was imagining it all,' she replied. 'And anyhow, I hoped it was all over with, and I'd never have to think about him again. It seems worse, somehow, never seeing him, knowing he's around. I can't help wondering what he is up to.'

'At least the police said that in most of these cases that's all they do.'

'Yes. Yes, I suppose so. I shall just have to wait until he gets tired of his little game and moves on, or the police get hold of him.'

She finished replacing the files and stood back to inspect the effect.

'Either way, I'm not having him dominating my life and controlling everything I do.'

It was odd, she realised all of a sudden, since Julia's frantic phone call, she had stopped being afraid. Instead she was angry, well and truly fired up and furious that Philip could keep on doing this to her. All the stress and the tiredness of the past few weeks seemed to have vanished, to be transformed into a restless energy that had made her return to work with gusto.

'That's the spirit,' Adam said as he set the printer humming away, printing out the pages he had been working on. 'It's weirdos like him that get the rest of us men a bad name.'

Llinos turned to him with a frown.

'I suppose. I hadn't thought of it before. I just felt everyone would think it was my fault, or that I even liked the attention.'

'Of course they don't. Nobody thinks that. No-one worth knowing, anyhow. It seems to me it has nothing to do with you. It's just some sick fantasy he has to play out, and you were just in the wrong place at the wrong time.'

'And fell for him,' she said, ruefully.

'Don't beat yourself up about that. It takes ages to get to really know someone. And didn't you say you were on the rebound from splitting up with your fiancé?'

'Who'd just been having an affair with his secretary.' Llinos winced. 'I do know how to pick them.'

'Hey.'

He went over to her and brushed a loose straggle of hair away from her face with a light gesture.

'These things happen. You should have seen some of my disasters. Now they were bad.'

'Really bad?'

'Really, bone-crunchingly, blood-screamingly awful, and with plenty of witnesses and the odd tabloid hack to follow the end of the mess. Why do you think I've now got this rule about not dating colleagues?'

She looked at him with a faint smile, wondering how she could feel so intensely jealous of women she had never met.

'Mind you, I always said rules were there to be broken.'

'Did you now?'

'Mm. Quite a rebel in my time, you know. It's why they always said me and fame, riches and respectability would never last.' His hand touched her face, and this time it lingered. 'Llinos . . . '

'I must get on.'

She stepped away from him.

'I'm sorry. That was stupid of me. I imagine that could go down as the bad timing of the century.'

'Just a bit.'

To his relief, she turned back towards him immediately with a faint smile. Just let him get his hands on that idiot who had turned her face so pale and pinched these past few weeks and placed those shadows beneath her eyes! But the worst thing he could do, he thought to himself, was to go all heavy on her.

If he sent her running away from him and away from the protection her friends could give her, he would never forgive himself. He forced himself to smile, and answer in a light tone, as if it were simply a matter of scenery design they were discussing.

'OK, rewind that bit. It never happened.'

He reached back to the printer and took out the finished pages.

'Look, I'll get out of your hair. We've got a first rehearsal with the kids this morning for the Christmas play so I shall definitely not be troubling you. King Arthur calls.'

He paused, hand on the door, and turned back for a moment.

'I promise I won't be so clumsy again, Llinos. But when this is all over . . . '

He gave an unexpectedly boyish grin.

'Well, let's say if you want to make a move on me I shan't be in the least offended.'

Llinos laughed as he vanished, his footsteps hurrying down the corridor towards the stage, glad there was no-one there to witness her scarlet cheeks.

'If this is ever over,' she reminded herself, the warm glow flooding through her chilling all of a sudden.

She had gathered enough information on stalking during those last months in London to have no illusions about her predicament. This could go on for years. Philip had been clever enough to keep out of authority's way. This was a much smaller place, but there were still plenty of tourists passing through all the time, plenty of strangers to hide amongst. And how did she drag Adam and the others into all this?

She shivered. The office suddenly felt very dark, and very isolated from the rest of the theatre. Making herself a quick coffee as a reasonable excuse for a break, Llinos locked the office door and made her way quickly along the narrow passage and into the auditorium.

On stage, rehearsals were in full swing. Llinos settled down next to Rhys, who was perched on a seat in the front row of seats putting the finishing touches to a large transparent fish.

'They're doing the Lady Of The Lake

bit,' he informed her. 'The kids are all the fishes as she rises up through the water. It's looking good.'

Above them, Adam and Mari were ushering the children from the special needs unit as they bent and swayed, each with a large model of a fish, or a piece of weed, on a pole, swirling around Cerys who, even in her paint-stained trousers and T-shirt, managed to look stunning as she wove the graceful figure of the mermaid in and out of the children, rising slowly until she was held high above their heads.

'She's very patient,' Llinos remarked in surprise, as the fish gradually moved from utter chaos to a semblance of a dance, with Alex zooming in between in his wheel-chair, a large dolphin held proudly above him.

'Cerys? Not bad. Actually, she's OK once she forgets her airs and graces and her dreams of being snapped up to star on the West End stage.'

He caught Llinos's raised eyebrows at the unexpected warmth in his voice.

'Oh, no! Don't even go there. Cerys and I — no chance, not in a million years. Besides, I'm not useful enough for her future prospects for her to even look at me twice. It's only Adam she's got eyes for at the moment. So if I were you, I wouldn't let grass grow under your feet in that direction.'

'Rhys!'

'Well, there's no beating about the bush. I've seen the way he looks at you. Even Cerys knows he doesn't even know she exists when you are in the room. Why else do you think she is making the most of her time up there?'

Up on the stage, Cerys was smiling, questioning Adam closely about her movements in the scene, holding Alex by the hand.

'She'll keep on plugging away at him, and there's only so much a man can stand,' he added, rather gloomily.

Llinos eyed him. He looked very young and vulnerable. With those mournful dark eyes of his, Llinos thought suddenly, he could probably have half the female population of his media course at his feet, if he gave them the chance.

'Well, she's a fool,' she said.

'And thank you for that vote of confidence,' he replied, kissing her hand with exaggerated gallantry.

'Don't be an idiot,' she returned, with a laugh.

'OK, but only if you help me with this cursed fish. The kids made it, but the fins won't stay on while it swims. I'm afraid there's nothing for it but to sew them on.'

'I'm no good at that sort of thing!'

'You can sew, can't you?' His smile teased her. 'All women can sew.'

'Rhys, I never put you down as being so sexist! And you mean you are such a macho man that you can't? And there I was, thinking you were a well-brought up modern man who didn't need to run back to mummy when his shirt buttons fell off.'

'Ah. So you have seen through my devious little plan to get you to do all the work. OK, I'll do you a deal. You sew the fins on that side, and I'll sew them on this. Then I'll let you get back to your filing and your financial wizardry.'

'That sounds fair.'

She looked up and found Cerys watching them both, Adam forgotten for the moment, and a frown on her face. Llinos smiled to herself. Maybe Cerys wasn't quite so indifferent to Rhys as she made out. Oh, well, it wouldn't do that young lady any harm to discover a potential rival in that direction, and if it also served to distract her from wafting her charms in front of Adam's nose all the time, well, then, so much the better.

Giving Rhys the warmest smile she could muster, Llinos took the threaded needle he was handing over to her and set about attaching the fin to the side of the fish.

When she looked up again, Cerys was back in the midst of rising between the swirling and twirling fishes once more, although, Llinos noted with some satisfaction, she didn't seem to be concentrating on her part quite so fully as before.

Time seemed to fly past as she sewed away, and the rehearsals on stage slowly took shape. Even when the last stitch had been put in place, she sat entranced by the scene before her. The children were all so proud of their cardboard and tissue paper creations, each painted in bright colours with kitchen foil and sequins glittering with each turn and twist of the fish on their long sticks. They all worked so hard, their faces glowing, but solemn, as they concentrated on fitting their moves to the music played from a tinny cassette player at the side of the stage.

'Great!' Adam clapped his hands as the fish came to halt once more. 'I think we're ready for King Arthur. Then it'll be time for a break.'

'That's me,' Rhys said, with a grin at Llinos. 'My only rôle in this is to stand at the side and look on in wonder. That should suit Cerys down to the ground. She might even hand me over Excalibur without braining me first.'

He hesitated.

'You can bring this one up, if you like,' he added, nodding to the fish at her side.

He smiled up at a small girl waiting shyly at the edge of the stage, holding one of the support workers from the school with one hand, and a stick with a very small excuse for a weed in the other.

'Bethan has been waiting for it very patiently, and the more hands the merrier.'

Llinos swallowed. She'd never tried anything like this in her life!

'I'm not sure,' she muttered, but Bethan was smiling at her expectantly, and Alex had zoomed towards her, waving his dolphin for her to admire.

'Good idea. What you might call hands-on experience,' Adam remarked from his position on the stage, as he rewound the cassette to the beginning once more. 'Do you the world of good after all that filing.'

Llinos smiled at the waiting faces on the stage above her, and stood up, lifting the fish on its pole.

'Well, if you put it like that,' she replied, making her way up to join them.

She was quite certain that once the music started and the dance began once more, she would be hopelessly lost, fall over, and make an utter fool of herself. But Bethan, with her hands firmly next to hers on the pole of the fish, seemed to know every move, and guided her without any mishap, in and out of the other performers.

After a few minutes, Llinos relaxed and simply enjoyed the movement and the colours as the Lady Of The Lake rose up between the fish to hand the magical sword of Excalibur to King Arthur waiting in awe at one side.

'Mmm. Nice cardboard,' Rhys remarked, dryly, inspecting the hastily constructed stand-in for a sword held in his hand as the music died away.

'Well, if you hadn't messed about so much and finished the real one,' Cerys retorted, irritated, but no-one was listening.

The children were giggling, and even the helpers were smiling as Rhys's joke released the excitement of the rehearsal into laughter. The next moment, the fish were safely stacked up at the side of the stage and everyone was settling down to orange juice and biscuits.

With a jolt, Llinos suddenly realised that it was fast approaching lunchtime and she had been away from the office much longer than she had intended. With a quick thanks to Bethan for showing her the dance, and a wave to the rest, she slipped away and back to her work.

As she reached the office she found the door was open.

'Oh, no!' she muttered to herself.

For Sara Bronski, or one of the other trustees, to find her taking long breaks with so much work to be done was the last thing she needed.

'Sorry about that,' she said as she walked briskly through the door. 'I was just helping with one of the rehearsals.'

'So I noticed.'

She stopped abruptly. In her haste she had gone too far into the room to shoot back out again, and there, in her chair at the desk, sat an all-too-familiar figure, idly going through her correspondence.

'Philip!' she gasped, in a strangled whisper.

8

Llinos turned back to the open door. She had been so certain it had been locked. How had he got in? But he had got into Julia's flat without her noticing, until she found the torn page in the address book. Llinos remembered this with a cold shiver running down her spine. The old-fashioned office door must have presented no problem.

'What are you doing here?' she demanded.

'I wanted to see you. You can do better than this, Llinos.'

He waved his hand around the half-cleared office.

'Working with a load of handicapped kids? Not exactly you, is it?'

'Special needs,' she corrected, quietly, through clenched teeth, but he didn't seem to hear.

'You had a career in London, with

really bright prospects. Everyone who knew you always said so. You shouldn't be throwing it away.'

He looked like the old Philip, lounging at ease in her chair, smiling at her with his blue eyes, ready to suggest something outrageous, like taking a last-minute flight to wherever the mood might take them.

'I needed a change,' she replied, warily.

She could still see the Philip she had fallen in love with — spontaneous, full of fun — but she wasn't falling for that again. She was also seeing the cool watchfulness of his eyes, as if he was determined not to let her out of his sight.

'Well, I've come to take you back.'

Had he heard nothing she had said? It was as if there had been none of the silent watching, and the following of her for months in London, as if he had never broken into her friend's apartment for clues as to her location. It was as if she was the unhinged one, rushing off on a whim to try an alternative lifestyle, instead of fleeing his obsessive following of her.

'I've got your things.'

He indicated a small case next to the chair. Even if she had not recognised it instantly, the label from their last trip abroad was still there, with her name plain to see.

'Where did you get that from?' she demanded.

'Oh, it's the one you always use.'

'But it was in the bedroom in my flat.'

'Oh, yes,' he replied calmly. 'It was easy to find.'

She hesitated. Maybe he didn't know the police were keeping an eye on her flat and the theatre. Maybe he had been spotted and help was already on its way. But from the cool look in his eyes she wouldn't bet on it. This Philip would take care not to be seen whether he thought the authorities were on to him or not.

As if from another world, the distant

sound of music began, accompanied by shouts and laughter, as the rehearsal resumed. Llinos swallowed hard.

There was no-one within shouting distance, no-one to hear her at all. She was on her own! Heavy in her trouser pocket lay the mobile she always carried with her. If she could just distract him long enough.

'And you want me to just drop everything and go?' she began.

'Of course. I can take you back to my apartment. You'll love it there. I know how much you like the river. Anything else you need we can pick up later.'

'I see.'

The hairs on the back of her neck were rising. The police had never been able to trace this apartment of his, any more than they had been able to trace his place of work, or Philip himself. For the first time, Llinos felt herself to be in actual danger.

At least here, amongst people she knew, and with the mobile in her pocket, she had a chance. The moment she got into his car, she had a feeling she would be trapped, with no way out. He was clever in his craziness. It would take all her wits and a stroke of luck to be able to call the police before he discovered her phone.

'Llinos, Adam wants to know if — oh, I'm sorry. I didn't realise — '

If this was her stroke of luck, it came from a most unexpected quarter. Cerys had stopped dead in the doorway, eyebrows raised at the sight of the good-looking stranger seated in the office chair.

'It's all right, Cerys. This is Philip. He just popped in to see me. He's from London,' she added, as casually as she could sound, but with her eyes wide and fixed on Cerys's face.

'Oh, I see.'

Adam had promised he had had a word with all of them, Cerys included, about Philip and the possibility he might turn up at the theatre at some point looking for Llinos. Surely Cerys must realise what was happening, and the danger they were all in! At least she was near enough the door to run for help, and there was a phone down the corridor. But Cerys did not appear to have taken the hint.

'I do love London, don't you?' she was saying with her brightest smile, moving farther into the room, and perching herself on the edge of the desk right in front of the stranger. 'I'm an actress, you know. I would just so love to work in the West End. Do you go often?'

'I'm not really into theatre.'

Philip was frowning at her, but clearly quite unable to resist the full-on attention of a pretty young woman.

'No? I'd have thought you were. I know Llinos loves it. I'd have thought any friend of hers would have just loved the theatre. I'm trying for a musical at the moment. It would only be a very small part, and maybe an understudy, but it could be my big break.'

If Cerys was one thing, she was certainly a good actress, Llinos suddenly realised. For all her airs and graces, Cerys could never be accused of being an airhead, and airhead was exactly the impression she was giving off at this moment.

She must have known who the stranger was the moment Llinos introduced them, yet she had barely batted an eyelid, and she was now monopolising Philip's attention as if she found him the most fascinating man in the world, her body casually, but carefully positioned between him and Llinos so that she was no longer in his line of vision.

Llinos thought quickly. Cerys had given her the chance to reach the door and run for it. She would have given anything to do so, but she couldn't leave her rescuer alone to face Philip's fury. Who knew what he might do if he discovered his plans to have Llinos back within his power had been thwarted.

Slipping her hand into her pocket, her fingers found the number one on her phone. The number stored was her emergency number, and would take her direct to the local police.

Cerys was laughing now, as if the man in front of her was unbelievably witty. Llinos pressed the button, and prayed he could not hear it dial. It was connected almost directly.

'How did you know I was at the Theatre on the Pier, Philip?' Llinos asked, as loud as she dared, praying that the listener on the other end of the connection could hear her and would know what was happening.

How long would it take them to arrive, and what would Philip try once he realised what she had done? She swallowed hard as Philip turned towards her. Cerys's intervention seemed to have knocked him off balance, and his surface of calm was more than a little ruffled.

'I saw you come in.'

'Were you following me then?'

'I was worried about you,' he replied.

'I'm fine where I am.'

'No, you're not. You don't understand,'

he replied, grasping her case and standing up. 'We need to leave here now.'

'Llinos is at work. She doesn't finish for another hour,' Cerys put in brightly. 'Perhaps you would like to come and look around the theatre while you're waiting. It's a fascinating old building.'

'I've seen it.'

He strode over to Llinos, and grasped her hand.

'We need to go now. I came to save you, Llinos.'

'Save me?'

For a moment, she thought this was part of his fantasy about her, that he meant her future, her happiness, her soul, even. But there was something urgent in his tone that sent a shiver down her spine.

'Llinos doesn't need saving,' Cerys said, with a smile. 'She's not in any danger.'

Even Cerys couldn't quite hide the alarm dawning in her own eyes.

'Come on, Llinos.'

It was as if Cerys had never existed, as if she were not in the room at all.

'We need to go now.'

She looked at him. His eyes were without expression. He was, she thought to herself, truly insane, capable of anything. Hard, cold fear gripped her. She prayed as she had never prayed before that the police were hearing every word of this conversation and knew he was in the theatre. Every moment she stalled him in his plans and kept him there would give them time to arrive.

'Philip, what have you done?'

'It's for her own good. You'd never have been happy here, or with him.'

'Him?'

Llinos frowned at him as if she couldn't possibly think who he could mean.

'The tall one. The flashy director. He's always in the paper with some girl or other.'

Very briefly, Llinos met Cerys's eyes. Only a few hundred metres away, Adam was finishing the session with the children. His voice floated up towards them. Just a few minutes more and they would be ushering the children out of the theatre and down the pier towards safety. If only they could keep Philip occupied for just a little while longer.

'Oh, you mean Adam, my boyfriend,' Cerys said, with a dazzling smile.

She gave a merry little laugh, as if Philip had just told the most amusing joke in the world.

'Poor boy! I've warned him about that unfortunate manner of his. I'm sure Llinos is far too sensible to fall for it at all, and, anyhow, she's already promised me to be a bridesmaid at our wedding, haven't you, Llinos?'

Stifling a choke at this outrageous piece of fantasy, Llinos nodded.

'I know he can give off the wrong message at times and it gets him into all kinds of trouble. Young actresses can be very impressionable, you know.'

Cerys leaned towards him once more, her smile wide and charming, and more than a little flirtatious.

'I'll just have to find a way to give him a taste of his own medicine, then, won't I, Philip?'

Not even Cerys's smile could distract Philip now, Llinos saw with a sinking heart. He stood up, brushing her would-be rescuer aside, and held out his hand.

'It was the only way,' he said, as if explaining the most logical thing in the world, and one that she must surely understand. 'We don't need this place, and this way they won't even try to look for you.'

'Why won't they look for me?'

Llinos heard the question come out in a strangled whisper. He seemed so sure of himself, as if there was only one way this could possibly end. But Philip seemed barely to have noticed the interruption.

'It can just be you and me together, Llinos,' he was saying. 'For ever, darling, just you and me. Just as you promised. Just as it ought to be.'

'I promised no such thing!' Llinos

snapped, fear and a sense of a net closing in on her, sending all her carefully mustered caution to the wind. 'And I'm not leaving here with you, Philip. Not ever.'

'What's that?'

It was Cerys, gazing towards the door. Smoke was trailing underneath it, through the gap where it was open, bringing with it the acrid smell of burning. Her eyes met those of Llinos. So that was what he had meant when he said he was going to save her. Whatever fantasy he was living through now, it was a deadly one.

'I told you,' he said, grasping her arm. 'We need to leave now.'

'But we have to warn the others,' Llinos protested.

'Come on,' he said, half dragging her towards the door, 'or it will be too late.'

'No, Philip!'

Anger gave her strength to pull herself away.

'There are children in there. They'll need to get the ones in wheel-chairs out to safety. I'm not leaving them.'

'Leave her alone,' Cerys said, grasping his arm.

He shook her off easily, and grasped Llinos round the waist, lifting her bodily and carrying her towards the door. Llinos bit and struggled and kicked for dear life, but his grip was like a vice, and he didn't seem to feel the blows she aimed at his shin. For a moment they tussled, twisting and turning as Philip carried, pulled and dragged her towards the door.

'Get off me!' Llinos yelled, tearing at the hands imprisoning her.

She managed to pull one set of fingers apart, and aimed for the narrow gap. But the other hand was still gripping her as hard as ever as she twisted, half falling to the floor, as the phone shot out of her pocket with an echoing thud. There was a moment's silence.

'What's this?'

Philip grabbed the mobile and put it to his ear.

'Who's that you've been calling?'

His face had turned pale and his hands were white at the knuckles. The time for trying to fool him was past.

'The police,' Llinos said defiantly. 'They'll be on their way by now.'

Llinos knew she would never forget the silence, as long as she lived. His eyes had gone still and cold. As far as he was concerned, she had betrayed him. His voice was hard.

'Then pray they'll be here on time,' he said, throwing the phone to the floor and crushing it beneath his foot.

The next moment, he had pushed past them, and through the door, locking it behind him.

She had broken free of him. In that moment Llinos knew it. She had shattered whatever spell she had ever had for him. As far as he was concerned, she could share the fate of the rest of those still within the theatre.

'He's cut the land-line,' Cerys was saying behind her at the desk. 'I'm sorry, Llinos. I was only trying to help.'

'I know, and you were brilliant. This is not your fault. I'm the one responsible for all this.'

'I can't hear any smoke alarms,' Cerys said.

'Trust Philip to be thorough. We've got to get out and warn them, or they won't have time to get everyone to safety.'

Smoke was now oozing in clouds under the door, with an ominous crackling sound in the corridor behind. There was only one other means of escape — the window.

'Come on,' Llinos said, pushing the desk against the wall beneath the window. 'I'm sure he never thought to check that the lock was broken.'

She pulled herself up on to the desk, and Cerys up after her.

'Good thing we don't wear skirts for this job,' she said. 'Come on, Cerys, let's get out of here.'

9

'You can do it, Cerys!' Llinos looked up from her position on the edge of the pier at her companion wrestling herself through the narrow gap in the office window high above.

Behind her, she could see smoke pouring from the theatre and drifting over the sea. There was only a narrow gap between the theatre walls and the railing for the pier. They would never make it past. She could feel the heat from here.

Llinos looked down at the surge of the tide around the metal supports of the pier. It could already be too late to make it round the side to safety. They might well have to swim for it. Above her, Cerys had wriggled her way through the gap.

'It's so far down,' she gasped.

'I'll catch you. Come on. The office

door won't hold much longer. Come on, Cerys, hurry.'

In the far distance, she could hear the sound of a fire engine, and then another. Through the smoke, she could even see the flash of red making its way along the shore. Help was coming! But supposing Adam and the others hadn't made it out in time?

She knew Adam would never leave Alex and the other children in wheel-chairs. With Philip's handiwork with the smoke alarms, they would have had no early warning. Supposing they hadn't got out on time?

Cerys wriggled around, lowered one leg gingerly, and then the other, holding on for dear life to the top of the window frame.

'Llinos!' There was panic in her voice, and in her face as she twisted to look down. 'I can't swim.'

'Well, I can. I'll do my life-saving technique if I have to. Come on,' she commanded, surprising even herself by the no-nonsense tone to her voice.

Cerys took a deep breath, and let go. Only just in time, Llinos saw, as she caught her. A roll of flame burst into the office, sending the windowpanes shattering, and showering glass all about them. Llinos held Cerys tight, pulling her down beneath the protection of the railings, and shielding her from the worst of the hailstorm of safety glass.

'OK?'

'Yes. How are we going to get out?'

'We'll have to swim.'

'But the others?'

Cerys looked back, as if contemplating an attempt to rush into the flames in a reckless attempt to reach the children inside.

'Look, they got out.'

Just for a few moments, a gust of wind parted the dark pall of smoke in front of them, giving the two a clear view of the pier.

'See, Cerys. They're making their way down towards the road. Adam got them out in time. They're OK.'

'Thank goodness for that,' Cerys breathed.

The wail of sirens drifted towards them from the shore.

'The fire engines are here. They'll have the flames under control soon,' Llinos said.

But her relief was short-lived. The fire engines might have arrived, but the flames above them were already taking stronger and stronger hold in the office above them. The heat was growing by the moment, and sparks shot out like fireworks every few seconds, to rain down on their faces.

Cerys had grasped her hand and was holding it hard. A piece of roofing snapped off and fell past them, sizzling into audible steam as it hit the water below.

'It could go at any moment. We'll have to jump for it,' Llinos said.

She leaned over the balustrade and looked down at the waves below. The sea was almost black in the greyness of the November afternoon. It would be cold, Llinos knew, and the tide, she could see, was on its way out. With its force, it would pull them away from the shore. It was not a tempting prospect.

As if in answer to her thoughts, a second piece of roof tumbled past, almost striking her cheek as it went, accompanied by an ominous cracking sound.

'Now, Cerys.'

For a moment, Llinos thought fear had totally overcome her companion, but Cerys was frantically peering between the clouds of smoke now settling around them.

'There are steps, down to the waterline,' she called. 'Adam said he used to go fishing from them with his uncle when he was a kid.'

'We haven't got time!'

'Yes, we have. It's just over there. Even if we have to jump, it won't be so far. Think, Llinos. If we're injured on the way down we haven't got a hope of surviving in that water. They're over here. I can see them. Come on! The farther we get away from the theatre the better.'

It was a long, slow climb down the narrow metal slats that formed the route down to the water. Llinos was aching by the time they reached the bottom, but at least they were protected by the structure of the pier from the burning masonry raining down around them. They could see more smoke, blocking out the sky, and between it, more fire engines rushing along the shore.

Llinos clung to the bottom step just above the reach of the waves and swallowed. The water looked even colder close-to, and the swell was high. In her heart she was not sure she could make it to the shore pulling Cerys as well, but did they have a choice? The metal around them might protect them for the moment, but the fire appeared to be raging just as fiercely overhead.

'I'm not sure we should stay here,' she muttered.

A wave broke next to her, enveloping

her jeans with icy water and making her gasp. A few steps above her, she could hear that Cerys's teeth were already beginning to chatter, while she could see that the fingers that clutched on to the metal rungs were white. A few more minutes and she would be forced to let go.

'Llinos!'

For a moment, she was quite sure she was dreaming, or at least hallucinating with the cold and the lack of oxygen due to the smoke. The voice came again, louder this time. Craning her head round carefully so as not to upset her precarious foothold, Llinos saw a familiar figure clutching the network of ironwork under the pier, with a large, bright orange ring, of the kind left on the side of the pier for emergencies. As she watched, Adam launched himself into the path of an outgoing wave, using its force to carry him to the metal joist next to hers.

'Thank heavens you're both safe,' he called, pulling himself out of the water and making his way precariously along a narrow metal bar towards them.

'Adam?'

Cerys slid herself down the last few steps until she was resting next to Llinos.

'He must have come right underneath the main part of the fire,' she said. 'The idiot!'

'You can say that again,' Adam said.

He braced himself as the next wave crashed against him, nearly dislodging him from his perch, before taking the last few steps to join them next to the ladder.

'I'm just glad you got out of there. The worst of the fire was in the corridor, so there was no way you could have got out. I was so afraid.'

He paused, but his hand clasped itself tight around Llinos as she clung to the structure.

'But you're OK.'

'And Rhys and Mari and the others?' Cerys asked anxiously.

'Fine, all of them. Mari was a

wonder. The moment we saw the smoke, she told the kids they were going to practise parading the mermaid and the fishes down the pier to the minibuses. She and Rhys had all of them, and the support workers, out of there before the flames really took hold. I dread to think what might have happened if she hadn't been so quick-witted and there had been a panic.'

'Good for Mari,' Cerys said. 'I wouldn't have kept my head like that,' she added, a little ruefully.

'Nonsense. You'd have done just the same, and you and Llinos had the presence of mind to get out of the office and get down here. I'm glad you did, I can tell you. I wasn't fancying that climb up there one bit.'

He released Llinos's hand to lash the ring firmly to the bottom rung of the stairway, before taking out his mobile from deep within his jacket.

'Good, the salt hasn't got to it yet.'

The next moment he was detailing

their position to the coastguard on shore.

'Damn,' he muttered as he finished the call and shoved the phone back into a pocket. 'They're saying it looks as if this part of the theatre could collapse at any moment. They're sending a boat out, but it looks as if we'll have to swim for it, after all.'

'But Cerys . . . ' Llinos began.

'Can't swim,' he finished. 'I know. Why else do you think I filched this thing under the firemen's noses before they had a chance to send me back amongst the civilians to tear my hair out with anxiety?'

He untied the ring.

'In you go, Cerys.'

'But what about you and Llinos?'

'Oh, don't worry, we'll be clinging to you like limpets, darling. I don't know about you, but I want to be right next to the brightest thing in the water and picked up as soon as possible.'

Cerys hesitated.

'But you'll face swimming lessons or

immediate dismissal from now on,' he added with a grin and Cerys gave a weak giggle.

'I'll do anything for you if we get out of this,' she replied, with an earnestness quite unlike her usual flirtatious manner and giving him a quick kiss on the cheek. 'You're my number one hero from now on, Mr Griffiths.'

She stepped inside the ring and pulled it up around her, before closing her eyes tight and launching herself into the sea.

'Ready?' Adam said, turning back to Llinos.

Above them the structure of the theatre creaked ominously. Llinos nodded.

'Don't worry if we start to go out to sea. We'll never make it back against the tide under our own steam anyhow. The main thing is to get as far away from the pier as possible, and then wait for the launch to pick us up. So just swim like the clappers and push Cerys out as far as we can go.'

His cold lips brushed hers.

'You OK?'

'Yes,' she whispered.

Just so long as he was with her, she didn't care any more what happened.

'Right. Come on then.' He clasped her hand. 'On three. One, two . . . '

The next moment, they were both engulfed by the cold sea, and swimming towards Cerys as strongly as they knew how.

10

The water was colder than anything Llinos had felt before. Huge surges of waves swept her this way and that, threatening to engulf her, or at least toss her out of reach of the orange lifesaver and into the vastness of the sea where she might never be found.

'You OK?'

She discovered Adam swimming strongly next to her.

'We need to get farther away. We're still too close.'

He guided her towards Cerys, who looked as small and frightened as a child within the orange ring.

'Come on!'

They swam as hard as they could, fighting the waves that attempted to fling them back towards the pier. Llinos concentrated all her efforts on pushing the buoyancy aid, her shoulders against its smooth sides, and her legs kicking strongly.

'It's going!'

She heard Cerys's shout as if from a far distance, and twisted herself around just in time to see the office end of the theatre sway in its envelope of smoke and flames, then pause as if not quite able to make up its mind, before collapsing into the sea. For a moment the water hissed around them with white-hot pieces of masonry, and then settled into quiet once more.

'It's all gone,' Llinos murmured, gazing at the blackened hole that had once been her workplace. 'There's nothing left. Nothing at all.'

She felt hot tears well up and spill on to the frozen skin of her face.

'And it's all because of me. It's all my fault.'

'Nonsense.'

In the waves, Adam's hand found hers.

'You weren't to know what the maniac would do. And you did your best to tell the police. I heard them say it was your phone call that alerted them so soon.'

'And you knew what Philip might do if he'd known what you were up to,' Cerys put in. 'If I'd had any sense, I'd have left when I had the chance, when you introduced us and I realised who he had to be. If I hadn't been playing heroics and thinking I could outwit him I might have been able to warn everyone in time.' She smiled. 'But I'm glad I stayed.'

Llinos returned the smile. With her hair darkened by water and plastered to her head, the finely-sculptured lines of Cerys's face had been thrown up into sharp relief. All of a sudden, she had ceased to be just another pretty blond and transformed into a timeless beauty.

'I'm glad, too,' she replied, 'even though I'm sorry you were scared half to death.'

'Oh, it's something I'm quite sure I shall use in my future glittering career,' Cerys returned, with an attempt at humour. 'Actors are supposed to be able to conjure up some strong emotion from the past when the characters they are playing find themselves in trouble. And I'll never complain the swimming baths are cold for the rest of my life.'

Llinos laughed, but across the cold water her eyes met Adam's to find a reflection of her own unease. Unlike the two of them, Cerys was not using her whole body to swim. Her hands were already white with cold, and her teeth had begun to chatter.

'The launch will be here soon,' Adam said, reassuringly, rubbing the hand nearest to his own. 'Just hang on, Cerys, it won't be long now.'

Llinos looked back again towards the pier. They were safely away from the immediate danger, but now they were too far. They had been caught in the currents and were being slowly but surely swept out into the sea. Philip might just get his wishes, after all. She could feel herself growing cold to the very core. Her mind was slowing, making every thought hard to grasp hold on to. And she was so tired, so tired! It would be so easy just to let go and drift.

'Llinos!'

She was aware of Adam grabbing her by the nearest shoulder and shaking her.

'Don't you dare,' he said firmly.

He lifted the hand that had slid away from the orange ring and placed it back on its taught and shiny surface.

'No drifting away, Miss Elliot, thank you very much, and leaving me here at the mercy of an irate employee. Wake up.'

Llinos blinked, and pulled herself back out of her stupor.

'Sorry,' she muttered.

'That's all right. Just don't do it again,' he replied.

He was very pale, she noticed with a clutch of fear. Adam had been soaked on his journey under the pier to rescue them, and had been battling the effects of cold for even longer than her or

130

Cerys. The pier seemed farther away than ever, while the distant line of the shore appeared barely visible. The distant howl of sirens reached her ears. Were they still attempting to put out the fire? Maybe the fire crews had arrived too late, after all, and the entire building had been destroyed.

'The puppets,' she muttered. 'All those beautiful puppets!'

'Don't worry about them.' Adam was doing his best to sound cheerful. 'At least the mermaid is safe, and the kids will just love remaking the rest of them.'

Llinos winced. Those weren't the puppets she had meant, but those old and precious puppets Sara Bronski had showed her as a child. They had been passed down from generation to generation of the Bronski family, along with the traditions that went with them. They were more of the heart of the Theatre on the Pier than the building itself would ever be. And now they were gone, in a moment, and all because of her.

Suddenly, she knew that, whatever happened, she couldn't stay. Hadn't she done enough damage already? How could she face Sara Bronski, who must surely hate her for causing so much destruction?

How could she face Mari and Rhys, and even Cerys, who had all worked body and soul to make the little theatre a success?

And the children. How could she ever face Bethan and Alex and all the others who would be deprived of their treasured performances and the parades along the pier, and whose very lives had been put in danger by that stupid love-affair of hers with Philip?

And Adam — she glanced over to where he was chatting rapidly to Cerys, demanding that she answered his every question in an attempt to keep her eyes from closing, as the effects of hypothermia began to set in.

Adam had given up everything to work at the Theatre on the Pier — a career, money, fame, and the freedom to do any theatre project he chose in the West End or on Broadway.

How could he ever forgive her? How on earth would she ever be able to face him again? Misery and guilt clutched her, colder, even, than the dark waters around her.

It seemed at that moment as if she had seen a glimpse of true happiness, and true fulfilment, and she had thrown it all away.

Whatever happens, she thought to herself, Philip will have had his revenge.

'You OK?'

She found Adam leaning towards her, one hand still clasped in Cerys's, and a worried frown on his face.

'I'll be fine,' she replied, with as much cheerfulness as she could muster, knowing they would never be this close again. 'And it can't be long now.'

As if in answer to her words, there was a roaring whine of a motor, and a flurry of spray, as the first launch reached them. Above, she could hear the drone of a helicopter making its way from the shore as their rescuers arrived . . .

A few days later, Llinos slipped out of her flat, locking the door behind her and leaving for the station.

'Dearest, are you sure about this?' Aunt Hannah frowned at her as they waited in the almost-empty station for the London train.

'The police have finished interviewing me for the moment, and they say at the hospital I'll be OK so long as I don't overdo things for a while,' Llinos replied.

'That was not what I meant, and you know it. I've had Sara Bronski on the phone several times, not to mention that nephew of hers. They are really concerned about you, Llinos.'

'It's very nice of them.'

'Nice?' Hannah almost exploded. 'I don't think nice comes into it. They're worried that you are all right. You've been through quite an ordeal, my girl. They only want to help.'

'I need to get away, be on my own,'

Llinos muttered.

Aunt Hannah grunted as if to express her doubts about this statement.

'Get away from what, exactly? People who love you and want to help you?'

'They must hate me!'

'Don't be ridiculous. You were nearly killed. Why on earth should they hate you?'

'Don't you see, Auntie? It's all my fault. I've destroyed everything.'

Aunt Hannah patted her shoulder gently.

'Things are never as bad as they seem, Llinos. Why don't you go and talk to Miss Bronski, or Mr Griffiths?'

'I can't,' Llinos muttered. 'I just can't.'

They sat for a moment in silence. All around them on the damp station, passengers were gathering with their rucksacks and their cases. Aunt Hannah sighed. The train would be here at any moment.

'Well, I'll keep an eye on the flat until your month's notice is up,' she said.

'Thanks, Auntie. I'll send up removal men once I've found a place in London.' She gave a rather wan smile. 'Julia has been wonderful, but I can't expect her to cram all my stuff as well as me into her spare room.'

'But you'll be coming back for the car, at least?'

Hannah frowned. Llinos stared along the line of the railway as the train came into sight. She was far too tired, and with her nerves taut as could be, to face a six-hour drive back to London, but she knew what her aunt was thinking. If Llinos was coming back to fetch her car, then it would give her a chance to see the place again with new eyes, and maybe change her mind before the month's notice on the flat ran out.

'I don't know.'

The train was almost upon them. Rucksacks were being hoisted on to shoulders and suitcases wheeled towards the edges of the platform.

'A car can be such a nuisance in London. Maybe I should just sell it.'

'Well, think about it first,' Hannah said. 'It'll be OK for a while in my drive. And you never know, my dear . . . '

Llinos took one last look back at the little town clustered around the beach and the promenade. She could make out the pier stretching out into the wide sweep of the bay, with the burned and blackened remains of the theatre standing forlornly at the far end, waiting to be demolished. There was no-one on the pier. Maybe there never would be again, she thought to herself, gloomily.

It had been cordoned off ever since the fire. The local paper had run several articles on the dramatic events and the tragic loss of the historic theatre, along with speculations that the structure was so damaged the pier itself might have to be dismantled.

A thirty-five-year-old man, believed to be from the London area, is helping police with their enquiries.

Llinos had cut out and kept each one

of the articles for that simple, almost throw-away last line. She held the sentence like a talisman, proof in black and white that Philip would never be able to follow her again.

If Julia hadn't made the discovery about the address book, and she hadn't confided in Adam, then Adam and Mari might not have had the presence of mind to get everyone out and as far away as quickly as possible at the first sign of trouble. And if the police had not had that prior warning, and the best artist's impression Llinos could give them, then Philip could well have successfully kept on sauntering down the pier just behind Mari and the children, as if he were nothing more than a member of staff. He could have melted away into the town, instead of landing fair and square into the arms of two burly constables and being whisked away to the cells of the nearest police station.

The train had stopped now. Doors slid open to disgorge passengers and take on a new load.

'Thanks for everything, Auntie,' Llinos said, giving Hannah a hasty kiss. 'I'll ring you when I get to Julia's.'

'And you take care of yourself,' Hannah replied. 'And no hasty decisions, mind.'

Llinos gazed back as the train jolted and slid away from the platform, gradually picking up speed. The waving figure of Aunt Hannah faded into the distance as they moved along the edges of the town, past the sad remains of the Theatre on the Pier, then along the coast until the sea and the mountains were left far behind.

I'll never, ever, be able to come here again, Llinos thought to herself, and the scene through the window blurred with her tears.

11

'Well?' Julia demanded, shaking the last of the April showers from her umbrella and stashing it in the hallway of her flat.

'They've offered me the job,' Llinos said, looking up from the letter in her hand.

'There, what did I tell you? They'd have been mad not to take you. It will be almost like having your old job back.'

'It's a different department,' Llinos replied absently, shrugging off her wet raincoat and running her hand through her damp hair.

'But we'll be working in the same building again.'

'At least I can start looking for a flat of my own and get out of your hair.'

'No hurry, Llinos. I've enjoyed having you here.'

'I'm not sure Danny would agree,'

Llinos returned, with a smile.

'Danny likes you.'

'And I like him, but it's you he's madly in love with and I'm quite sure he would mind having you all to himself at weekends.'

'Not if that means pushing out my best friend.'

'I suppose I'd better ring them and accept,' Llinos said.

She felt Julia send a sharp glance in her direction and pulled herself together. She should be over the moon, jumping for joy, cracking open the champagne. She had just landed herself a brilliant, demanding, well-paid job with prospects, and as near as could be to the one she had been forced to leave with a heavy heart less than a year ago.

'No hurry,' Julia said. 'It's too late, anyhow. No-one will be there. They'll know you wouldn't get the letter until you got home from work, so they won't be expecting an answer until Monday.'

She was silent for a moment, fiddling with the clasp of her handbag, as if trying to make up her mind about something. All of a sudden the fiddling stopped and she opened it up with an air of determination.

'But I think we should celebrate. I've got tickets for the theatre for us tonight. Macbeth. I know you've been dying to see it.'

'But it was sold out months ago!'

Julia tapped the side of her nose in a conspiratorial manner.

'I just happened to do a favour for an old friend.'

She held up the two tickets.

'I'll have you know these are rarer than gold dust, so you'd better cram yourself into your best dress, Cinderella, before the pumpkin arrives.'

Llinos giggled. A night out would do her good and she would have two whole days to think about the job and what she was going to do.

'But what about Danny?'

'Oh, don't worry about Danny. He's got a gig in a pub in Hammersmith tonight, last-minute thing. The other

142

band had a double booking. He said he'd meet us for a drink in the bar beforehand, if we get our skates on.'

Llinos eyed her suspiciously. Julia already had her phone in her hand. Was this to confirm to her love-lorn boyfriend that the two of them would meet him later, or to ask him to make himself scarce for the evening?

'OK,' she said.

'Great stuff.' Julia beamed at her. 'I'll let you hog the bathroom first. Only don't take too long about it. I want to get there before Lady Macbeth starts murdering everyone.'

Llinos had a quick shower, while Julia seemed to spend an interminable time on the phone, no doubt unable to tear herself away from whispering sweet nothings to Danny, Llinos thought with a wry grin. On the other hand, she could be blackmailing every eligible bachelor within driving distance to make a foursome for the pre-Shakespeare drinks.

Oh, well, it wasn't the first time she

had tried. Over the past few months, Julia had paraded any number of available young men before her friend, without much success. Llinos didn't mind if she made another forlorn attempt tonight. She was used to her friends efforts by now, and as long as Julia didn't press the second ticket into the chosen swain's hand and vanish into the night on the back of Danny's motorbike, there would be no harm done. It might even be quite fun. Julia did have very good taste in eligible young men, Llinos had to admit! At worst, the evening would prove a distraction.

The two young women arrived at the theatre in plenty of time, even a little early, by the emptiness of the foyer, and the bar staff deep in preparations for a hectic evening ahead. Live music had been laid on to entertain the pre-theatre drinkers.

'Oh, good,' Julia said, appearing particularly pleased with herself. 'We can have a look around before it really gets crowded. I must dash to the loo then I'll see if they're ready to serve us some drinks. There's an exhibition up on the next level. I've heard it's a real must-see. I'll meet you up there.'

Without giving her friend a chance to reply, Julia vanished into the soft gloom at the edges of the subtle lighting of the foyer. Well, she could hardly stand there on her own in the middle of the arriving theatregoers like some idiot who had been stood up by the love of her life! Llinos turned and made her way up the short flight of steps to the upper floor of the theatre.

There she found a series of large display cases almost entirely filling the space between the entrance to the stalls. Llinos blinked, and then cursed her friend under her breath. She'd known Julia was up to something! In the first case there was a display of shadow puppets, used, so the label informed her, for the telling of traditional stories in a Hindu temple in India. Intricate patterns had been stamped into the wafer-thin leather allowing the light to glow through and shimmer on the bright tints of red and gold decorating the stylised figures, with their elegant headdresses and long, fine fingers.

Llinos gasped. They were so beautiful, and so loved, and well used. She could almost imagine the children watching in awe as stories of gods and goddesses, of princesses crossed in love and brave heroes unfolded in the flickering light of small candles.

She looked up at the banner above her head and read, **Theatre in the Community**. She glared at the letters with an impulse to wring Julia's neck now, this minute, but she found she was already stepping past the Indian shadow puppets, drawn into the rest of the display.

For a while she was dazzled by the bright colours around her. African masks stared down from a backdrop of hunting lions and dry savannah. A Viking longboat stood waiting, surrounded by photographs showing how it would be set alight and allowed to drift out to sea in a replica of a Viking funeral. In the next case, she was almost dazzled by a huge headdress from the Notting Hill Carnival, which shimmered like the exotic display of a peacock, surrounded by photographs of each stage of the making, and the final figure dancing in the middle of the procession.

Llinos stopped, unable to move. She was going to disgrace herself and cry, she could feel it. In a moment, she had been taken back to the Theatre on the Pier, with the children making the outsized mermaid and the brilliantly-coloured fish, excitedly preparing their performance in the theatre and the procession through the town after afterwards.

Julia was quite right. How on earth could she go back to wheeling and dealing financial deals, and clawing her way up the corporate ladder, when her heart was still in the Theatre on the Pier? She might not be able to go back,

but there were other community theatres working with disadvantaged children.
She could stay with the temp agency
and volunteer with one of them, and
then take some proper training.

'Spectacular, I agree. But a bit
ambitious for us, don't you think?'

Llinos froze at the familiar voice in
her ear.

'Adam! What on earth are you doing
here?'

'The same as you, admiring the
exhibition. I've heard it's a really
must-see event.'

'I bet you have.' She scowled at him.
'This wouldn't be from Julia, by any
chance?'

'Well, now you mention it . . . '

'I knew she was up to something. I
just didn't think she'd stoop so low.'

She squared her shoulders and
clenched her fists.

'Well, go on then. Say what you have
to say.'

'You make it sound as if I'm about to
bawl you out. A little bit out of place

with the genteel ambience, don't you think?'

'Well, I'm not going anywhere else,' she replied, stubbornly. 'So you might as well get on with it.'

'As you wish. But I'm afraid, my dear, that what I have in mind just might get us thrown out of the place immediately.' He took a step towards her. 'But, of course, if you insist.'

'Don't you dare!'

Llinos took a step back. More people were beginning to drift into the exhibition by now and one or two were eyeing the pair with open curiosity.

'Go away, Adam. Leave me alone.'

'Well, I'd like to say that your wish is my command but since I have tickets to the play, I can't very well leave.'

'You can't have! It's all booked out,' she blustered.

'Ah, but then the director is a very good friend of mine,' he returned with a smile. 'I managed to get my hands on several as it happens.'

'So that's how Julia . . . ' She came to

a halt and glared at him. ''Favour for an old friend,'' she said. 'I might have known what she was up to! What are you doing here, Adam?'

'Being a knight in shining armour.' He grinned as she began to scowl again. 'Oh, not to you, Llinos, much as I would wish it. I brought Cerys down for her audition for a part in The Lion King.'

That brought her down to earth with a bump.

'That was nice of you,' she mumbled feebly.

She swallowed hard. So Cerys, without her airs and graces, had got what she had always wanted after all. She looked up to find Adam frowning at her.

'No, it wasn't, and don't go putting two and two together and making two thousand and ten. I'll have you know I don't change my mind that easily, my girl. If I hadn't had a very ulterior motive, young Cerys would have had to fend for herself on the train this morning. I've had one member of staff run out on me already. I'm in no mood to lose another one. Oh, and before you ask, she got the part. So that will mean Rhys will be taking up that post-graduate media course at London University he has been muttering about for the past few weeks, and I'll be down to just Mari.'

'But there isn't a theatre any more.'

'For an astute businesswoman, you can be remarkably dense at times.'

'I beg your pardon?' she snapped indignantly.

'Have you never heard of insurance?'

'Well, yes, but — '

'The structure of the pier wasn't damaged, despite all those horror stories in the Press. The Victorians certainly know how to build things to last, you know. We've been given the run of the town hall until the new theatre is finished. I hate to say it, but this has generated more publicity for us than we have ever had before. I suppose it takes the loss of something for people to realise just how precious it is. We've had firms offering to donate materials and services and the committee has been swamped with offers of help. With that and the insurance, we'll have a modern, state-of-the-art community theatre before you can turn around. All we need is an administrator to keep everything in order and make sure we make the most of all this publicity.'

'But the puppets. Those beautiful, old puppets from Miss Bronski's family! Because of me they were destroyed and they can never be replaced.'

'Julia said those puppets were worrying you, Llinos. Why do you think I persuaded her to lure you here?'

Llinos frowned at him.

'You don't think we still kept those puppets in the theatre, do you? They are far too valuable, real collector's items. Any thief with half a brain would have them out of there and on the way to New York before Mr Punch could say sausages. They're usually in the local museum in Llaneilwyn but they've been on tour for the past year.'

He grasped her hand and pulled her through the rest of the exhibition until they came to a large case set up as a traditional marionette theatre.

'They're all there!'

Llinos stared at them, her eyes blurred with tears. There were the puppets she remembered so clearly from her childhood, all poised on their strings as if ready to spring into action at any moment.

'They're all safe!'

'Of course they are, Llinos. They've been travelling around with this exhibition and causing quite a stir, I can tell you.'

'But the theatre was still destroyed, Adam. I could have killed you all.'

'That wasn't you, Llinos. From what I can make out, Philip wasn't even interested in harming the rest of us. All he wanted to do was to have the office so badly burned, everyone would assume you had died in the fire, so that by the time forensics had decided there was none of your DNA amongst the ashes, he would have got you stashed away somewhere you would never have been found.'

Llinos began to shiver. She had woken up like this, night after night, shaking from head to foot from the nightmare. This time she found strong arms around her, holding her tight.

'You didn't destroy the Theatre on the Pier, Llinos. Philip did that. A theatre can be rebuilt, even better than before, but if it had been you he had succeeded in destroying, well then, I don't think I could have borne it.'

They stood for a moment, until even Llinos, with her head resting content-edly on his shoulder, oblivious of everything else in the world but her own happiness, became aware of the stares they were beginning to attract.

'I think they believe we are under the impression the play is *Romeo And Juliet*, not a blood-curdling murder story with ghosts and witches,' she murmured into his ear, gently detaching herself.

'We can always find a quiet park instead,' he replied with a grin.

'Certainly not, Mr Griffiths. If you think I'm going to miss the chance of being able to swan in on the arm of the sexiest man in the place, you've another think coming.' She smiled sweetly. 'Besides, I've had a crush on the actor playing Macbeth for years and I have a feeling we'll be going backstage after the performance.'

'No way!' Adam replied. 'The man's lethal. He can spot a pretty woman at one hundred paces and he doesn't care whom she is with. I'm sure Cerys would have had a whale of a time. I'm sure she'd have provided a wonderful distraction. Pity, really, I brought Rhys down to hold her hand while she waited for the decision. Last I saw of them, they were off to hit every nightclub in town. And I'm afraid you might find your friend, Julia, is all set to sail off into the night on the back of a motorbike in the general direction of a certain Irish pub in Hammersmith. So I'm afraid it's just you and me.'

'Then I shall just have to hang on tight,' Llinos replied.

'Well, in that case, I might just be persuaded to take you to meet the cast afterwards, so long as you don't let go.'

'Oh, no problem,' Llinos said with a smile.

12

Along the sea front, the parade was all set to go. It was a beautiful summer day, with not a cloud in the sky.

'Ready, Alex?' Llinos asked.

Alex nodded, his eyes travelling up once more to rest proudly on the dolphin above his head, anchored on a pole attached to his wheel-chair. Already crowds of summer visitors, attracted by the unexpected sight as well as the brightly-coloured posters scattered around the town, were gathering to watch.

'OK,' Adam called, standing next to Sara Bronski at the head of the procession, his hair wild and a suitably harassed expression on his face. 'I think they're almost ready for us.'

'And about time, too,' Mari muttered, who had been helping the two new puppeteers hired to replace Cerys and Rhys, as they struggled to contain the excited children for the past half hour. 'Just how much time does it take to get a mayor in position with a brick and a trowel?'

'I don't think it's the trowel so much as the Press and the film crews,' Llinos replied with a grin. 'This is more publicity than the town has had in the past fifty years, so they've got to get it right.'

Mari laughed.

'I don't know how you got them all here, Llinos.'

'Oh, you know. **Children's Theatre Rises from the Ashes** makes such a good headline, besides my charm, and never letting them forget us for the past few months. I'm sure they came just so they didn't have me nagging them over the phone yet again.'

'And because you are a genius,' Mari replied.

Llinos smiled, and was about to send back a jokey comment in return, when she caught the glint of tears in her friend's eyes.

'Mari!'

'It's all right.' Mari sniffed, blinked hard, and gave Llinos an abrupt hug. 'I'm just glad you're here, that's all. When I think what might have happened.'

'Well, it didn't,' Llinos replied firmly. 'I blamed myself for so long, but then when I realised the police had been looking for Philip for years, I realised just how very charming he could be and how believable he was. And all I can think now is that he knew how to spot someone who was feeling low and vulnerable, just as I was after that horrible break-up with Robin.'

'And at least you saw through him in time,' Mari said.

'Yes. That's something I'll be thankful for all my days,' Llinos replied. 'I realise now that I was one of the lucky ones.'

She shivered, the familiar rush of cold travelling down her spine as it did whenever she thought of Philip and what he might have done to her had Cerys not barged into the office that day and been so quick-witted and brave, and risked her own life in the process.

There had been a string of unsolved murders, stretching back over a decade, all of them young women who had recently broken up from a long-standing relationship, and who had told their friends a few months later how wonderful it was to be swept off their feet by a romantic and successful businessman who was so eager to take them to exotic places. No wonder the police had been so delighted to have him in custody at last. Philip had been very careful not to leave behind any evidence of himself, or traces of DNA, but the last few times, he had grown a little less careful, perhaps assuming arrogantly that the police would never be able to catch up with him. Philip, she was certain, would never be free to walk the streets again and watch her from the shadows with those cold blue eyes of his.

'Look, they made it in time!' Mari exclaimed, distracted by the sight of Cerys and Rhys, arms entwined tightly around each other, waving encouragement from the crowd.

'Come and join us!' Llinos called.

'Are you sure?' Cerys asked.

'Of course! You'll always be part of the Theatre on the Pier,' Llinos replied. 'And, anyhow, we can do with all the help we can get.'

'Wonderful.'

Cerys made her way towards them, looking, Llinos noted with a smile, more elegant and radiant than ever.

'Hi, Cerys, hi, Rhys. Glad you could make it.'

Adam had left his position at the front of the group and appeared beside them.

'How are the bright city lights?'

'Great. I wouldn't have missed it for the world.' A faintly wistful expression crossed Cerys's face. 'But this here is very special.'

'Cerys has been helping out at a community theatre in London in her spare time,' Rhys put in. 'Once you've got the bug, you see, everything else seems so shallow.'

'The theatre is not shallow,' Cerys retorted, who still, it seemed, could not help rising to Rhys's bait. 'And anyhow, you're the one aiming for Hollywood.'

'Just because I want to work in films does not mean I want to high-tail it off to Hollywood,' he retorted, following her as she made her way towards the head of the waiting children. 'There are plenty of film projects working with disaffected teenagers.'

They vanished, still squabbling amiably.

'I think that is true love, you know,' Adam said, watching them go with a thoughtful expression on his face.

'I think you're right,' Mari replied.

Up in front, the band began to play.

'At last!' Adam muttered, running his hands through his hair. 'I thought they were going to keep us here for another hour at least, and with all those kids champing at the bit to get going.'

'You're not going to lead us, then?' Mari asked.

'No, thank you. I'm leaving that honour to Aunt Sara. She is the right one to face the cameras and be on the front of the newspapers tomorrow morning. I've made the excuse of catching the stragglers. Not that there will be any, I'm quite sure.'

'Oh, right. I see,' Mari said. 'Nothing to do with the fact that that is supposed to be Llinos's job, I take it?' Her smile broadened. 'Come on, Alex, our turn now. Let's get that dolphin really leaping for joy.'

'Such a fuss over one brick,' Adam muttered. 'I'm sure they could have finished half the theatre with all the time and effort it took to organise all this.'

'Rubbish. Think of the publicity, and, anyhow, see it as a thank you to the mayor and the town for being so helpful.'

'Ever the practical, rational one. What on earth would we do without you?'

'Flattery will get you nowhere, Mr Griffiths.'

'Really? Come to think of it, I'd been meaning to talk to you about that.'

'So just how long will you be this time?'

They both swung round as the Punch And Judy man brushed past them, the habitual scowl on his face.

'An hour at the most, but the last bit of that will be all the media doing their thing, which won't interfere with your performances,' Adam replied, good-humouredly. 'It'll be over before lunch time. You're very welcome to join us, John.'

'Hrmmph,' he grunted. 'Business,' he muttered.

'Oh, but think of the publicity,' Llinos said brightly. 'I'm sure the Press will be anxious to interview you as a representative of such a long history of puppetry tradition. And besides, I'm sure they'll be dying to have shots of you entertaining the children on the promenade afterwards. What do you think, Adam?'

'No question of it. In fact the BBC was on to me just yesterday about the rôle of traditional performers in community theatre. Their man is over there, next to the ice-cream van.'

As if bowing reluctantly to overwhelming pressure, without another word, he dived back to where his assistant was setting up their little booth.

'Now, as I was saying,' Adam resumed, turning back to Llinos, but at that moment, the music grew to an ear-splitting crescendo.

The parade around them began to move, sweeping them along with it, crowds of onlookers joining behind them as they began to make their way towards the laying of the first brick of the new Theatre on the Pier.

'Come on,' Llinos said, linking her arm in his. 'Let's just enjoy the moment. This is the beginning of a new era, Adam.'

'New!' the Punch And Judy man snorted scornfully, as he passed them by at a rapid trot, Mr Punch and his dog at the ready to greet the man from the BBC, with a long line of sausages trailing behind them in the wind!

With the ceremonious brick laid, and the media's curiosity largely satisfied, the procession made its way back to the town hall, where a celebratory party was soon in full swing.

'Look, can we get out of here?' Adam muttered, extricating Llinos from a very animated woman from the Arts Council. 'I've had an overdose of suits and bigwigs for one day.'

'I was networking!' Llinos protested.

'Well, you look all networked out to me. How about we ditch the orange juice and the champagne and go for a cappuccino on the front? Or better still,' he added thoughtfully, 'an ice-cream on the beach. I want to have you all to myself, for a change.'

They found a quiet spot amongst rocks that gave some protection from the wind, but which still allowed a reasonable view of the pier.

'That's better,' Adam said, finishing his cornet and leaning back against the nearest rock. 'Now we can finish that conversation we began earlier.'

'We can?' Llinos said. 'What conversation was that then?'

'The terms of your employment.'

Llinos blinked in surprise.

'I know everything has been far too busy these past few months to really talk, and I felt you needed some space after what happened.'

'I know,' she replied. 'And I've been more grateful than you could ever have imagined.'

'I just hope you appreciate how much restraint I had to put myself under all these months not dragging you out for moonlit walks and candlelit dinners.'

'I thought you didn't date colleagues on principle,' Llinos reminded him with a smile.

'I don't. Bad idea altogether.'

'Adam, if you are thinking of sacking

me just so we can go out for a cappuccino, you've got another think coming!' she returned indignantly.

'Sack you? Oh, I couldn't do that. After all you've done to get the Theatre on the Pier back on its feet again, Aunt Sara would never forgive me.'

'You're not going to leave, are you? I thought you liked working here.'

'Oh, I do. I've no intention of going back to working in a commercial theatre again, which leaves us with a bit of a problem.'

'Does it?'

'Of course it does. I can't work with you a moment longer without making a serious move on you.'

'Really?' Llinos leaned a little closer to him. 'Well, that is a relief, because I can't work with you a moment longer without making a serious move on you, and I know you once told me you wouldn't mind in the least, but I'm not sure just how that would translate into practice.'

'I don't know. You wouldn't like to try it out, would you?'

'No, I wouldn't,' she replied with a giggle. 'I'm afraid I'm an old-fashioned kind of a girl.'

'Ah, well, there's only one thing for it. You'll just have to marry me.'

'What did you just say?' Llinos stammered.

'Llinos! I'm asking you to be my wife! Aren't you supposed to faint, jump for joy, start arguing about bridesmaids, or something? Not just sit there looking at me so seriously like that.'

'You caught me by surprise, that's all.'

He sat up, frowning indignantly.

'How can it possibly come as a surprise that I love you, adore you, and can't live without you?'

'I nearly killed you,' she murmured, the laughter gone from her face.

'No, you didn't. Some seriously sick madman tried to do that. It had nothing to do with you. Well, as near nothing to make no difference to me. Not that it would anyhow. Nothing could ever change how I feel about you, Llinos.'

'Oh,' Llinos said.

'Well? Do I have to prove it? I'll do anything, Llinos. Anything to prove to you that you can trust me, and that we were meant for each other. I'm afraid it will take an entire lifetime to prove how much I love you.'

Llinos felt a warm wave of happiness rush through her.

'Well, there is just one thing you can do,' she said.

'Anything!'

'You can kiss me.'

'Ah,' he said, his frown replaced instantly by a reflection of her smile. 'So does that mean you might love me just a little, and you'll consider marrying me, so that I can't possibly be said to be dating you?'

'Of course it does, you idiot,' she replied. 'I love you, and I trust you with all my heart, and I want nothing better than to marry you and live happily ever after. There, now are you going to kiss me?'

And, of course, he did!